PRAISE

MW01505794

"An emotional roller coaster of a finale that will leave readers exhilarated."

—*Publishers Weekly* (starred review)

"A love story that's as messy, funny, and unapologetically complicated as real life."

—Nikki Payne, author of *Sex, Lies and Sensibility*

"Sexy, flirty, and fun, this romance entranced me from the first page."

—Ashley Herring Blake, *USA Today* bestselling author

"Alexis Daria gives us all the delicious tension readers crave."

—Julie Soto, *USA Today* bestselling author

PRAISE FOR *A LOT LIKE ADIÓS*

"A charming, sexy spitfire of a novel!"

—Emily Henry, *New York Times* bestselling author

"The steamy love scenes, vibrant cast, deeply felt emotions, and sense of fun make this a surefire hit."

—*Publishers Weekly* (starred review)

"A must-read for those who love contemporary queer, family-focused romances."

—*Library Journal* (starred review)

"Second chance romance perfection!"

—Tessa Bailey, *New York Times* bestselling author

PRAISE FOR *YOU HAD ME AT HOLA*

"Sexy, compelling, and complex—a terrific romance from a rising star of the genre."

—*Kirkus Reviews* (starred review)

"An absolutely pitch-perfect summer escape."

—*New York Times* (editor's choice)

"A triumph of Latinx joy and feminist agency."

—NPR

"I could not get enough of Jasmine and Ashton!"

—Jasmine Guillory, *New York Times* bestselling author

PRAISE FOR *TAKE THE LEAD*

"This perfect romance will dance its way into the reader's heart."

—*Kirkus Reviews* (starred review)

"A sparkling debut."

—*Entertainment Weekly*

"Vibrantly written."

—*The Washington Post*

"Stone and Gina's chemistry leaps off the pages . . . A must-read!"

—Mia Sosa, *USA Today* bestselling author

THE
HOLIDAY
Hookup
LIST

ALSO BY ALEXIS DARIA

You Had Me at Hola

A Lot Like Adiós

Along Came Amor

Only Santas in the Building (novella)

What the Hex (novella)

Amor Actually (anthology)

Take the Lead

Dance with Me

Dance All Night (novella)

THE
HOLIDAY
Hookup
LIST

ALEXIS DARIA

Montlake

This is a work of fiction. Names, characters, organizations, places, events, and incidents are either products of the author's imagination or are used fictitiously. Otherwise, any resemblance to actual persons, living or dead, is purely coincidental.

Text copyright © 2025 by Alexis Daria
All rights reserved.

No part of this book may be reproduced, or stored in a retrieval system, or transmitted in any form or by any means, electronic, mechanical, photocopying, recording, or otherwise, without express written permission of the publisher.

Published by Montlake, Seattle

www.apub.com

Amazon, the Amazon logo, and Montlake are trademarks of Amazon.com, Inc., or its affiliates.

EU product safety contact:
Amazon Media EU S. à r.l.
38, avenue John F. Kennedy, L-1855 Luxembourg
amazonpublishing-gpsr@amazon.com

ISBN-13: 9781662534157 (paperback)
ISBN-13: 9781662533952 (digital)

Cover design by Caroline Teagle Johnson
Cover image: © Anna Efetova / Getty

Printed in the United States of America

For the "Sorrows. Prayers." group chat, because this story is too spicy to dedicate to any of my relatives.

Chapter 1

VALENCIA

I am what some might call a workaholic. At least, my ex-fiancé sure liked to throw that word around, but this isn't about him. It's about me, Valencia Torres, a lawyer at the New York City office of the Environmental Protection Agency. Besides, does it really count as being a workaholic if you're fighting to save the fucking planet? Have you *seen* the latest climate change projections? Implementing large-scale clean-energy initiatives is like rolling a massive boulder up the side of an active volcano, but if I can push that rock just a smidge further and buy humanity a little more time—whether we deserve it or not—all the long hours I spend at the office will be worth it.

So yeah, I work a lot, and I won't apologize for it. Not even to a certain professional hockey player who tried to use my job as an excuse for why he cheated on me.

During the rare moments when I'm home, you can find me curled up on the sofa with a cozy mystery, a glass of red wine, and my old gray cat, Archimedes. Archie's fifteen years old and hated my ex from day one, so he's obviously a better judge of character than I am.

The sofa is my favorite spot in the whole apartment. It's mustard yellow, and I've covered it with colorful throw pillows and the two blankets I crocheted during a failed attempt to find a hobby. Unfortunately, this couch has seen better days. Archie shredded the sides long ago, and the cushions sag where Everett used to sit. I know I'll have to toss it when I move, but I don't want to think about that.

Tonight, I'm going out.

My best friend Fern invited me to a holiday-themed dance party in Brooklyn. I said yes, despite my plan to skip all things Christmas, because this is the first time in years I won't be spending the holiday with Fern and her family. Besides, I love dancing, so I'm going to live it the fuck up tonight.

Just because I'm a bit of a homebody doesn't mean I don't know how to get dressed up. My makeup is immaculate, with contouring, smoky eye, and a bright red lip. I flat-iron my hair to within an inch of its life and pull it into a high bun so I don't sweat all over the back of my neck. And in the bottom of my jewelry box, I find a pair of gigantic sparkly snowflake earrings.

Now I just need an outfit.

My nice dresses have been gathering dust in the back of my minuscule closet, although they did get some play this summer during my "Hookup Era." A few months after Everett and I called it quits, I downloaded all the apps and went out with a bunch of men and women. The most promising was Anton, a professional soccer player. What can I say? I have a type, and it's men with broad shoulders, fucked-up knees, and compulsively disciplined workout regimens.

Anton and I had an extremely satisfying three-week affair before he and his giant dick moved to Europe to join a team. I went on a few more first dates but cut them all short by pretending to have a work emergency. Then, because the universe and the federal government like to play games, I actually *did* have a work emergency, which led to months of frustration that my team has only recently managed to emerge from. With all that going on, dating has been the last thing on my mind.

And if sometimes I feel the tiniest bit lonely while sitting on my couch with Archie, a book, and a glass of wine, well . . . I don't want to think about that, either.

I wrestle my bland, business-casual attire out of the way before delving into the dark recesses of my closet. A flash of color jammed between two nearly identical little black dresses catches my eye.

It's a formfitting, cranberry red halter dress I bought for some fundraising event I went to with Everett after he joined the NHL. He thought it was "too sexy," and I ended up renting a floor-length gown instead. But for tonight? It's perfect.

The hem hits a few inches above my knee. Wide straps cross over my chest and shoulder blades, leaving my arms and most of my back exposed. Despite what Everett said, it isn't *too* revealing. And I feel good in it. *Really* good. Not at all like myself.

And honestly, even I'm a little bored with myself these days.

Since it's nearly sixty degrees outside, I forgo tights and tug on high black boots with medium heels. See my earlier comment about climate change.

After stuffing a tiny purse with necessities, I slip on a lightweight wool coat and wave to my cat on the way out.

"Farewell, Archimedes. Mama's gotta go shake her ass."

Archie blinks at me from the sofa, then resumes licking his back. I leave the hall light on for him.

One taxi ride over the Williamsburg Bridge later and I'm in front of Dazzler, a queer nightclub in Bushwick. The building is unassuming gray brick with a pink neon sign. A trio standing near the door catches my eye. One is dripping in silver and pale blue crystals, a snowflake-encrusted tiara perched atop a wig of tumbling white curls. A drag Snow Queen, perhaps? Next, a muscular figure wears reindeer antlers and a BDSM harness. Their red ball gag is reminiscent of Rudolph's nose. The third sports a red and gold nutcracker jacket and holds a bag—or a *sack*, if you will—labeled DEEZ NUTS.

I snort. But then my stomach sinks. Something tells me I'm underdressed. Or *over*dressed, if the reindeer's leather thong is anything to go by.

All three of them are talking animatedly and fanning themselves, paying me no mind as I pull open the door. Once inside, I pay the cover, check my coat, and forge ahead to look for Fern.

The club is dark, lit only by flashing red and green lights. Mist from a fog machine crawls up the walls, giving the packed space an eerie vibe. Or maybe that's just the sexy Grinch, complete with facial prosthetics, voguing on the bar. High above, two acrobats wearing nothing but glitter and red booty shorts writhe and spin on giant hoops suspended from the ceiling.

I find Fern dancing by the stage, where a DJ pumps out a steady stream of Christmas pop song remixes.

Fern breaks into a smile when she sees me, and her amber eyes light up. "Valencia! You made it." She grabs me in a tight hug and kisses my cheek. "I'm so proud of you for coming out tonight."

I give her a squeeze, and when I step back, I raise an eyebrow at her furry white bikini. "Did you skin a yeti?"

"Oh, shit, I forgot my ears." She rummages in her massive purse and pulls out a set of rabbit ears stuck to a headband. "Guess what I am."

She puts them on and does a little spin. Her short, bleached blond hair flares out around her heart-shaped face, and her septum piercing glints in the strobe lights.

It takes me a moment, but then it hits me. "A snow bunny. Cute. The tail is a nice touch."

She waggles the fluffy pom-pom on her butt. "I thought so."

Her friends arrive bearing shot glasses. All of them are similarly decked out as sexy snow bunnies.

"You didn't tell me there was a group theme." I try to keep the hurt out of my voice as Fern hands me a snowball shot.

Fern clinks her tiny glass to mine. "You're always busy with work. I didn't want you to feel like you had to make a costume."

She knocks back the shot and I follow suit. It's minty, with a hint of chocolate, and it slides down my throat with a cool burn, leaving me tingling and sort of edgy. Or maybe it's just Fern's words that set me off.

Sure, I *am* busy and I'm *not* crafty, but shit, I could've bought something. Not that I particularly *want* to dress like Beach Mode Cruella de Vil in the middle of December, but it would've been nice to be included instead of feeling, once again, like Fern's boring lawyer friend.

I glance around at the mass of sweaty, writhing, mostly bare bodies surrounding us. "I just didn't realize there was a dress code."

She frowns. "What do you mean? You look great."

"I look like I came from my office Christmas party." I don't know why I'm belaboring the issue. Short of stripping down to my underwear, there's nothing I can do about it.

But Fern squints as she scans me up and down. Then her face brightens, and she digs around in her purse. A moment later, she slaps something into my hand. "Here. Try this."

It's a coiled string of tiny LED lights.

"Who are you, Mary Fucking Poppins?"

She just laughs. "Put them on."

"Um . . . how?"

"You know, just . . ." She makes a vague swirling motion with her fingers. "Wrap them around yourself like you're a sexy Christmas tree."

I examine the white plastic battery pack attached to the end of the lights. "Where am I supposed to hide this? My dress doesn't have pockets."

She taps my chest, right between my boobs.

"But I'm not wearing a bra!"

"Good, they're a tool of the patriarchy."

"No, I mean, it's going to fall out."

Fern snorts. "Not with your magnificent tits. Tuck it in and you'll see."

I have my doubts, but I slide the plastic case into my cleavage while Fern winds the string of lights around my upper body. When she's done, she steps back as much as she's able to and studies her handiwork. "Perfect. I should send a picture to Ev so he sees what he's missing."

I groan at the mention of Everett. "Please don't."

She winces. "You're right. My idiot brother doesn't deserve to see you like this."

Okay, yes, it is a *little* awkward to be besties with my ex's younger sister. But despite being a chaos demon who lives to stir shit up, Fern has always had my back. For instance, after she found out Everett was cheating on me with one of his fans, she forced him to tell me the truth. That's what gave me the kick in the ass to do what I should've done ages ago.

I can't believe it's been almost a year since then.

No. No more thinking about Everett. I look amazing, and I *will* enjoy myself tonight, goddamn it.

After a quick adjustment to the lights spiraling up my arms, I grab Fern's hands and we dance like our lives depend on it.

And you know what? It's *fun.*

Except I'm definitely overdressed. The club is practically steaming, and I'm *parched.* But the crowd around the bar is at least three deep, and I don't feel like wading through all those bodies just for a vodka cranberry.

Part of me feels like I'm too old for this, but shit, I'm only twenty-seven.

Maybe I'm just tired. Good thing I put in for vacation time over the holidays, although I need to spend it packing.

"Ow! Santafucker!"

At Fern's exclamation, my head snaps around. "What's wrong? And did you just say—"

"Yeah, I did, and—*shit*." She grimaces in pain as she balances on one leg. "I twisted my ankle."

"Here, hold on to me. Can you put weight on it?"

Gingerly, she sets her foot down and gives a relieved sigh. "It hurts, but I can walk a little."

"I'll help you get home." I move to slide an arm around her, but she wags a finger in my face.

"Nuh-uh. You never go out anymore, and I'm not letting you leave early because of me."

"I really don't mind." I pull out my phone to check the time. "I've already been here . . ."

"A grand total of forty-five minutes." Fern shakes her head. "No, Valencia. Stay. Drink. Dance. That's an order. Mwah!"

And she's gone.

Around me, the party rages on.

Well, hell. If this is the only Christmas thing I'm doing this month, I suppose I should make the most of it. Patting the battery pack between my boobs for good luck, I push through the crowd toward the bar.

Chapter 2

GIDEON

One drink. I came to Brooklyn for *one drink*, and only because it's Rodrigo's birthday and he's my self-appointed "work husband."

After we finish the first round—paid for by me, as usual—I'm getting ready to leave. But then Rodrigo's boyfriend, Bailey, insists that everyone check out the party down the block at Dazzler, so off we go.

The two of them don't miss a beat. The second we arrive, they both strip to the waist. A random person smears body glitter on their bare chests, and now they're dancing under the strobe lights like happy disco balls. Me? I don't know what the fuck I'm doing here. I ditched my suit jacket, but I'm wearing a tie, for Chrissakes, while everyone else is dressed as anthropomorphic candy canes or whatever. I'm more of a leather-armchair-and-whiskey-neat sort of guy, and yes, I realize this makes me sound approximately sixty years old instead of twenty-seven.

Fuck this. One *more* drink, and then I'll wish Rodrigo a happy birthday, call for a car, and hit the treadmill in my building's fitness center for a quick and brutal run so I can actually sleep tonight.

But as I approach the bar, I realize "one more drink" is easier said than done. It's an absolute shit show. I peer over the festively attired masses, searching for a break in the crowd, when—

Holy fuck.

The club is loud, dark, and smells like bodies and beer, but everything fades away as my eyes land on the shapely brunette trying unsuccessfully to flag down a bartender.

The back of her red dress shows more smooth beige skin than it covers, and lights twinkle like fireflies around her upper body. Her ass is, frankly, out of this world, but that's not what consumes my attention. Not all of it, anyway.

Her black hair is pinned up, leaving her long, elegant neck exposed. My gaze fixates on the arch of her hairline where it meets her nape, and I'm gripped by the sudden and intense urge to taste her *right there*. My lips tingle as I imagine kissing her skin, slow and deliberate, before closing my mouth over the column of her throat and dragging my tongue along her soft, warm—

Shit. Where the fuck did that come from? My pants are tight, just from staring at some unknown woman's neck. I haven't felt desire this strong in months. Not since . . .

Since my father died. Since I started therapy. Since I broke up with Christina. Take your pick.

I let out a shaky breath. Nothing like thoughts of your dead dad and your indifferent ex-girlfriend to make your sex drive slow to a crawl.

But it's still there. Like a craving. I haven't even seen this woman's face yet, but the way she's standing on tiptoe and waving her arm, trying desperately to order a drink, is kind of adorable.

I have to talk to her. She'll probably turn me down— either with scorn, laughter, or a polite, *Oh, honey, no.* Hell, she probably doesn't even like men. We *are* in a gay bar, after all. But if nothing else, Ralph will be proud of me for trying.

And I'm definitely not going to think about why I want to make my therapist proud. Or how it mirrors my relationship with my father. Nope, not thinking about any of that.

Focusing on *her* helps me ignore the sensory overload of the club as I move forward. Even in heels, she barely comes up to my shoulder, and she's having a tough time getting the attention of either of the two bartenders.

Stepping up behind her, I lower my voice. "Excuse me. Can I get you a drink?"

She plants her hands on her hips and makes a disgusted sound before she turns. "You're certainly welcome to try. I swear, I've been at this for a full five—*Noble*?"

Her dark brown eyes widen and her mouth hangs open in shock. At the sight of her familiar face, my mind goes blank.

It's Valencia Torres. My former classmate.

Former target.

Former *obsession*.

The corners of her lips tug upward in a disbelieving smile. "Gideon Noble, is that you?"

Kill me now. "I—yes."

Her pretty mouth twists as she crosses her arms. "Well, well, well. If it isn't my old archnemesis. What are you—" Realization dawns over her features. "Oh, my God. Were you *hitting* on me?"

"No. Of course not." I say it quickly. Too quickly.

She raises a perfectly arched eyebrow. "Are you sure?"

I want to kiss that sarcastic smirk off her face.

Fuck. Where is this *coming* from?

All right, I can admit it. Torres is fucking stunning. She's come a long way from the wild-haired suck-up with caterpillar eyebrows I knew back when we were both students at Carlton, a private school on the Upper East Side. It's almost unfair how incredible she looks. But while the smirk on her red-painted lips is new, the knowing glint in her dark eyes is the same.

I clear my throat and try to dispel thoughts of kissing *Valencia Torres*. "It just seemed like you were struggling. To order a drink, I mean."

The smile drops from her face as she glances back to the bar. "They're totally slammed. I don't know how they're managing with only two bartenders on a Friday night."

She's turned away from me. This is my chance to sneak off and try to put this out of my head until my session with Ralph next week. God, he'll have a fucking field day with this.

Thinking of Ralph reminds me that I don't run away from things anymore, and I'm hit with a bolt of clarity.

What if, somehow, I'm being granted the opportunity to make up for all the bullshit I put Torres through back in middle school? What if this is my chance to interact with her the way I wanted to in high school if I hadn't been so fucking scared?

Before I can begin to imagine what that might look like, Torres spins around and grabs my forearm. Her eyes sparkle like obsidian in the flashing lights. "I love this song."

I'm instantly glad I didn't run away if it means I got to see her looking at me like this. Like she's okay with touching me. Like she doesn't hate me.

But then her gaze turns appraising as it sweeps me from head to toe, taking in my hair, my face, my clothes.

Her perusal makes me sweat. "Why are you looking at me like that?"

She squints at my shoes. "I'm judging you."

"And what's the verdict?"

I expect a response like, *Guilty as charged.* Instead, she gives a decisive nod. "You'll do."

"As?"

"A warm body." With a teasing grin, she tugs me away from the bar. "Dance with me, Gideon Noble."

I go with her, because if this is our second chance, I'm not going to waste it.

Chapter 3

Valencia

I can't explain what possessed me to ask *Gideon Noble* to dance with me. Or rather, *forced* him, since I didn't leave him much choice. He was clearly mortified once he recognized me, and it's possible I used that to my advantage. Still, he could've pulled his arm out of my grip or dug in his heels if he didn't want to come. The man is a foot taller than I am.

He's also . . .

No. The asshole doesn't deserve compliments.

But he really is . . .

Ugh. Fine. He's gorgeous. *Objectively.* His wavy hair is shorter than when we were kids, each strand perfectly styled in a classic side part. It's hard to tell in this lighting, but it looks darker now, more of a light brown than a dark blond. His narrow face has filled out, and his jawline better supports the wide lower lip that used to look bratty and now looks . . .

Bitable.

Yikes.

In the strobe lights, his eyes flash red, green, and red again. Mine are probably doing the same. I wonder if he notices.

I want him to notice.

Despite his denial, I *know* he came over to hit on me, and it makes me feel powerful. Electric. *Alive.*

He allows me to tow him onto the dance floor without complaint. And when I slide my hand down his forearm to his wrist and pull him toward me, he complies.

The heavy bass pounds through me like a second heartbeat. Between the driving vocals and the living pulse of the crowd surrounding us, I'm swept into the dance. I sway my hips and shimmy my shoulders. Noble's grip on my hand is tight as he spins me. His other hand splays against the bare skin of my lower back, firm and warm, as he takes over.

Noble is a *good dancer.* That's as much a shock to my system as his touch. He doesn't just nod his head to the downbeat, and he's not jumping around like a fool, either. He's *smooth.* He has actual rhythm. You'd think I would know that, but I can't recall ever seeing him like this at school dances.

And yes, damn it, I was looking. He only *acted* like a troll.

Plus, he *smells* good. Subtle but expensive. Woodsy, with notes of citrus and bergamot.

Why, why, *why* does he have to be so fucking sexy?

This started as a lark. A simple way to get back at him for years of torment. To make him uncomfortable and snag myself a convenient dance partner in the process. But there's something really hot about knowing that he's into me. Maybe it's perverse, but I want to drive him fucking wild.

Workaholic, homebody, nerd—all that might be true about me. But I can also dance my ass off, and Gideon Noble doesn't stand a chance.

I'm barely looking at him, keeping my eyes closed or my head turned away. But I'm hyperaware of every touch of hands, every brush of fabric, every graze of limbs. I pull out the heavy artillery—body rolls, hip swivels, spine arches. The quick glimpses I get of his face reveal hooded eyes and parted lips.

Mission accomplished. I'm seducing my former nemesis, and best of all, I don't actually give a shit what he thinks, which is freeing in a way I never could've imagined. Embracing it, I give myself over to the music, the melody, the movement, and just *dance*.

As this song melds into the next, Noble's hands grasp my hips, pulling me closer. My back is to him, with barely a breath between us as I raise my arms and gyrate to the music. The heat of his body radiates against mine, as erotic and intimate as his fingertips digging into the sensitive spot under my hip bone.

We don't say a word. But whenever our eyes meet, something hot and crackling passes between us.

I'm melting. This wasn't supposed to happen, but I don't want to break the spell.

A guy wearing a trucker hat and ratty cargo pants approaches me. He's drunk, the sloppy leer all but sliding off his generically good-looking face. Noble shoots him a dark glare and growls, "Fuck off."

The guy fucks off. I laugh and keep dancing.

The song changes and Noble spins me to face him. His gaze is locked on mine as he drags his teeth over that sumptuous bottom lip.

It takes every ounce of my self-control not to pull him down so I can bite it, too.

God, who *am* I?

There isn't even a breath between us anymore. His hands mold over my ass to swivel me to the rhythm of the music. His cologne invades my senses, and his dick is hard against my belly. I'm pushing into him, way more than I would if I were dancing with a complete stranger. But despite the fact that I haven't seen Noble in nine years, I know him. I saw him every single day from sixth through twelfth grade. And while we've never been this close, never touched like this or moved like this, there's something familiar about him all the same, something that draws me in. The beat thumps in my blood, making me feel hot and a little reckless.

Maybe a *lot* reckless. Time will tell.

The next song has a slower rhythm. I step back and take a moment to fan my face, catch my breath, look away from the fire in those hypnotic green eyes. Somehow, my attempt to beguile him backfired, and now I'm the one in his thrall.

Before I can say something to erase the intensity of the moment, Noble grips my elbow and propels me toward the bar.

"Come on," he grinds out. "Let's get you that drink."

Chapter 4

GIDEON

I flash the bartender a hundred-dollar bill between my fingers, and we receive our drinks immediately. Thank God, because I need to cool the fuck down.

Three songs. That's all it took to make me wish Torres and I were alone, instead of in a crowded club. To make me wish we were different people with a less complicated past.

It started out innocently enough, but with her soft breasts pressed to my chest and her tight butt filling my palms, I got hard and couldn't hide it. She didn't seem to mind, though. If anything, she pressed closer, her dark eyes glued to mine with desire simmering in their depths.

Or maybe that's just wishful thinking on my part.

There's a small seating area separate from the dance floor, and it's blessedly devoid of strobe lights and humans. We carry our drinks to a vacant table in the corner with two battered wooden café chairs.

Torres perches on one and crosses her legs. My eyes follow the line of her boot up to her bare knee. I imagine tugging down the zipper and sliding her boot off, closing my fingers around her delicate ankle, spreading her thighs, and—

Fuck, I need to get a grip.

She eyes me over the rim of her vodka cranberry as she toys with the tiny straw. "So is this where we sit and reminisce about the good old days?"

And with that, my arousal plummets.

"Shit." I take a slow sip of my whiskey. "Nothing good about them."

She raises her eyebrows, like she's surprised by my answer. "No?"

I shake my head and change the subject. "What have you been up to?"

We're both lawyers, it turns out, which gives us something easy to talk about. But whereas I'm working in finance, she's an environmental lawyer.

As we chat, I recall the last time I teased her. We were around fourteen. I came across her in the school library, sitting alone at a table with a laptop open in front of her, surrounded by books and papers. I can't remember what I said, probably something tired and trite. She didn't even look up from her notebook as she declared, "Go fuck yourself, Noble. I'm busy." Her dismissive tone struck me and made me realize—for the first time, I'm ashamed to admit—that *I* was the asshole in this situation.

After that, I might've tried to talk to her a few more times, innocuous comments about class or homework, but she'd responded with the same bored indifference she used when I'd been mocking her, and my fragile teenage ego couldn't handle it. I barely talked to her through the rest of high school. There was one moment of weakness at graduation, and then . . . nothing.

Until now.

She's telling me about a project involving the Clean Water Act, when a crowd of scantily clad North Pole elves piles into the room. Torres is forced to scoot her chair closer to mine, and I get a clearer whiff of the sweet citrus scent that so tantalized me on the dance floor. I lean in for a deeper inhale and pitch my voice over the raucous laughter coming from Santa's helpers.

"What are you doing here, anyway?" I ask, bringing the conversation back to the present moment. "Doesn't seem like your scene."

Her lips purse. "No?"

"Not unless they're hiding the *Beauty and the Beast* library in the basement."

She tilts her head back to chuckle, and I stare longingly at the line of her throat.

Blinking, I drag my gaze upward to her face.

She's stirring her drink with a rueful smile. "Fern invited me, and I like to dance, so here I am."

A tendril of dread unfurls in my gut. "Fern . . . Mulholland?"

"You think I managed to find another friend named *Fern*?"

It takes all my effort not to wince. I remember the Mulhollands, of course. Specifically the brother. Man, we hated each other back at Carlton. He was disruptive in class and always doing dangerous shit on his Rollerblades for attention.

But Torres . . . I glance at her left hand. There's a thin silver band on her pointer, but nothing on the ring finger.

I take a sip to clear my throat. "And you?"

"And me . . . what?"

"Not . . . Mulholland?"

"Oh! Um, no." She busies herself stirring the ice. "Still Torres. Everett and I broke up earlier this year."

"I'm . . . sorry?" It's a question. I'm obviously *not* sorry. But I don't know what else to say. We're getting into dangerous territory here. It was easier on the dance floor, where we could let our bodies do the talking. But it's impossible to act like we're two people who just met, who don't have the history we share.

She drains the last of her vodka cranberry and passes me the empty glass. "I need another drink if we're going to continue this conversation."

I leave to get us another round. But by the time I return, the moment has passed, and I don't know how to get it back.

"This doesn't seem like your scene, either," she says after I sidestep a sexy Krampus and take my seat.

"You don't like my costume?" I gesture at my wilted button-down shirt and tie. "I'm Corporate Businessman #2, here to turn the local Christmas tree farm into a strip mall."

Torres huffs out a genuine laugh, then gives the lights strung around her neck a light tug. "Well, in that case, it's better than my half-assed attempt to fit in."

Because I'm aching to tell her how fucking pretty she looks, I backtrack instead. "So why isn't this my scene? Because it's a club?"

She gives me a searching look. "Because it's a gay club."

She puts a slight emphasis on *gay*. Might as well tell her.

"It's not my first. I'm bi, Torres."

"Wait, really? Me too!" Her face lights up, and I'm relieved, but then her expression turns thoughtful. "Actually, I lean toward identifying as pansexual. It fits me better. I just didn't know *you* were. Not that I needed to know!" She holds up her hands, like she's worried she's offended me. "I mean, we haven't seen each other since high school, and obviously it's not

25

the kind of thing you need to broadcast. And I shouldn't have assumed that you were . . ."

"Straight? It's okay. I was kind of quiet about it until this year. Thanks to, ah, therapy."

"You're in therapy?" I expect her to sound shocked, but she sounds more intrigued.

I shrug. "After my father died, it turned out I had a lot of shit to unpack."

She grabs my hand and her remorse is obvious. "I'm so sorry, Noble. I hadn't heard. And I shouldn't have said it that way. You've clearly worked on yourself, and you don't deserve to have it thrown in your face."

"You'd be justified in throwing a lot more in my face, Torres, starting with that drink. I was fucking awful to you."

I can't suppress the bitterness in my tone, and her eyes shutter. She lets go of my hand, leaning back in her chair as if putting space between us. "I don't think I'm ready to go there yet."

Inside, I'm cringing. Whatever was building between us, I've just ruined it. But I swallow down the words I owe her and hang on to the one suspended in the air between us.

Yet.

We aren't there *yet.*

At some point, maybe there will be enough easiness between us, enough trust, for me to apologize. To explain.

We're already closer to that point than I ever thought we'd be.

I hear a song come on in the main club and set down my half-finished drink. Rising to my feet, I take her hand.

"What are you doing?" Her eyes are shiny when she looks up at me, but she doesn't pull her hand away.

I keep my tone even. "*I* like this song."

She doesn't say anything, but I catch the ripple of her gorgeous throat as she swallows. Then she nods and lets me help her to her feet.

Back on the dance floor, it's so packed we can barely do more than sway against each other, but any awkwardness that came up has dissipated. Torres's ass is pressed tight to my crotch, and I've got my arms wrapped around her waist, almost possessively. I half expect her to push me away, but one of her hands grips my wrist, as if holding me in place.

I duck my head, closing my eyes as I inhale the scent of her hair, like sweet coconut and tart lime. I can't get enough. It's going to haunt my dreams. In that red dress, she's like living fire in my arms, and I don't care that I'm going to get burned.

When the next song begins, she turns to face me and shouts over the music. "It's too crowded in here. I think it's time to go."

Go? My pulse trips, spurring me to act. I ignore the churning in my gut and lean down, my lips brushing her ear as I speak. "Can I take you home? It's late."

Even though hundreds of people are pressed in around us, it's like we're alone. She stares at me for a long moment, the lights reflecting off the disco ball overhead and glittering in her eyes like twinkling stars. No, like a whole goddamn galaxy.

Then, to my surprise, she says, "Sure. We could, um, finish that conversation."

I nod like it's no big deal. "All right."

Inside, my heart fucking soars.

Chapter 5

VALENCIA

We collect our coats, but I don't put mine on. I'm overheated, either from dancing or from the thought of bringing Noble home with me—probably both. On the sidewalk, we run into Noble's coworker, Rodrigo, who breaks away from a larger group to stand with us. Noble introduces me as his "friend from school," and I don't contradict him. *This is the girl whose life I made a living hell* would invite a lot of questions I'm sure neither of us feels like answering.

Rodrigo is medium height with tan skin and dark brown waves, and his boyfriend, Bailey, is my height, with light brown skin and glossy black curls. They laugh and brush body glitter off each other while Noble frowns at the rideshare apps. But when Rodrigo shortens my name to Val, Noble is quick to correct him.

"She doesn't like being called Val."

"Oop. Sorry, honey. I don't blame you. Valencia is a beautiful name."

I wave off Rodrigo's apology, but the exchange unnerves me. My mom's name was Valerie, and it made sense for people to call *her* Val. But the beginning of Valencia doesn't even sound like "Val."

It's also extra painful to be called by my mother's nickname now that she's gone.

But that's not what unsettles me tonight. No, the question rattling around my mind is, how the hell does *Noble* know that?

Rides are scarce, so Bailey suggests a bunch of us split a car back to Manhattan. I do a head count, then catch Noble's eye.

"Go with your friends," I say in a low voice. "I'll take the subway."

His nostrils flare in annoyance. "Torres, I'm taking you home, and I'm making sure these clowns get back, too. Don't fight me on this. You won't win."

There's no reason why his irritation should turn me on, and yet here I am, holding my coat to my chest to cover my hardening nipples.

"Well, it appears I am overruled," I say lightly, and give Noble my address.

I expected Noble's friends to be a bunch of cocky finance bros, but to my utter amazement, they're *delightful*. Rodrigo ruffles Noble's hair, which the latter permits with a long-suffering sigh. Bailey playfully sings the "Man in Finance" song at Noble, which pulls a laugh from me.

I still haven't fully decided why I'm bringing Noble home with me. To talk, sure. He seems to have something he needs to say, and I'd rather do it in the privacy of my apartment.

But I can't dismiss the feeling of his erection pressed into my abdomen. Or the blatant way I ground against him while staring into his turbulent green eyes.

When a black SUV pulls up to the curb, I give myself a shake and climb into the cramped back row. Noble follows and settles in on my right. His body is big and warm, and the scent of his cologne surrounds me. It's such a tight fit, we have to fasten each other's seat belts. The others cram into the seats in front of us. The overhead light flicks off, casting Noble and me in relative darkness, relieved only by brief yellow flashes from streetlamps as the car rolls through Brooklyn.

He leans down to speak in my ear, pitching his voice low under the sounds of classic R & B and his friends' laughter.

"Are you comfortable?"

The ghost of his breath on my neck makes me shiver. I wish I'd put my coat on, even though I would've been roasting.

"Mm-hmm. I'm fine."

I'm so far from fine it's not even funny.

Noble shifts next to me, repositioning his long legs, and I feel bad.

"You didn't have to squash yourself back here, you know. Bailey could've sat next to me."

Noble gives me a look I can't decipher. Sort of stern, a bit glaring, and very hot.

"Torres, I'm not letting anyone else squash in next to you. Not even Bailey."

"Okay." I'm finding it hard to breathe normally, a condition which is not improved when his gaze drops to my lips.

"I liked dancing with you." He says it so quietly I almost don't hear him, but I'm watching his mouth, too, and I see his lips and tongue form the words.

"So did I."

I utter the admission before I'm even aware I thought it. My mind is clouded, not from alcohol but from *him*.

Then his hand lands on my bare knee, big and strong and *scorching*. I want to feel his hands on every inch of my skin.

Before I can think better of it, I part my legs.

Not much. I'm not sitting in the back of this SUV with my legs wide open and a neon sign proclaiming TAKE ME NOW, GIDEON NOBLE! Just a few inches, but that, and maybe whatever is showing on my face, gives him the go-ahead to glide his hand a little higher. His fingers caress my inner thigh, and my breath catches.

"*Valencia.*" He utters my first name like it's a prayer or an oath, and I respond in the only way that makes sense.

I grab his tie and yank him down to kiss me.

And then, *finally*, that captivating lower lip is mine. I catch it between my teeth—gently, though, testing and tugging, learning its shape and suppleness with my tongue. Noble makes a tortured sound in the back of his throat that I swallow. I could spend hours exploring this lip, and it wouldn't be enough to fully map its mysteries. But I'm too impatient for that, and I stroke my greedy tongue deeper into his mouth.

Then it's my turn to groan, because holy fuck, he tastes *amazing*. Like whiskey and spearmint. And he *feels* amazing. Like a sex dream come to life.

Noble cups my jaw and proceeds to make good on the promises his body made on the dance floor, which I'm only now beginning to comprehend. *I am going to turn you inside out,* his kiss says. *I'm going to completely upend your world.* I surrender to the unspoken demand, and our kiss devolves into a frenzied tug-of-war of probing tongues and nipping teeth.

It's still not enough.

When his hand slips just under the hem of my dress, I whimper. "*Touch me.*"

I can't believe I'm saying this, *doing* this. In the back seat of a car full of strangers! But I'm so enflamed, I wouldn't care if all the patrons from Dazzler were watching.

His other hand lands on my breast, and while I meant for him to touch me somewhere else, that works, too. I arch into the warm pressure of his palm.

"What the fuck is this?"

I laugh at his confused growl. "Battery pack. Ignore it."

He does. And since I'm not wearing a bra, there's only the thin material of my dress between his stroking thumb and my nipple. I gasp, and he uses that to take the kiss deeper. God, his mouth is so fucking *dreamy*. I'm frantic for more.

My right hand slides up to cup his neck, and I drop my left directly onto the bulge in his pants. He jolts, but I don't let him break the kiss, not even when he moans hungrily into my mouth. Between the seat belt and his perfectly tailored trousers, I can't get a decent grip, but I can feel enough to know I won't be disappointed.

Because I've already decided I'm going to have sex with Gideon Noble. I think I knew it back on the dance floor when I let him feel me up. Or maybe when I took his hand and dragged him away from the bar.

Or maybe it was before that, the second I turned around and saw his handsome face, almost a decade older but still familiar, morphing from a seductive smolder to a nearly comical expression of shock and dismay.

Before I can make a half-assed attempt to talk myself out of it, Noble chooses that exact moment to slip his hand farther between my thighs. The tips of his long fingers brush the lace covering my mound, and now I really *am* sitting with my legs wide open in the back seat of a car.

But as with his pants, the seat belt and the hem of my dress conspire against me, and all we can do is grope and make out as the car takes us over the Williamsburg Bridge, across Lower Manhattan, and up to my apartment in the West Village.

"We're here!" a cheery voice calls out.

I pull away from Noble with a gasp. Rodrigo and Bailey grin at us over the backs of their seats. Disoriented, I blink out the window at the familiar four-story redbrick building, its stair rails twined with garlands of fir and pinecones, a large wreath hanging on the front door. Bailey hops out of the SUV and lowers his seat so we can exit.

"Ah, thanks." I gather my coat and purse as Noble unbuckles us. "Who should I pay?"

Rodrigo chuckles. "Gideon's paying. Aren't you, lover boy?"

"Out, Torres." Noble grabs my hips and propels me ahead of him. I nearly trip over his long legs.

My face must be beet red as I say goodbye. Noble climbs out and mutters something to his friends, who hoot and holler. And then the door slams shut, the SUV pulls away, and Noble's hand is on my lower back, guiding me to the steps of my building.

The breeze chills my heated flesh. My fingers tremble, though not from cold, as I pull out my keys and let us in.

We climb one flight of steps to my unit. At my door, Noble's hands grip my waist. His lips trace up the back of my neck.

"I've been wanting to do this from the first second I saw you." He breathes the words into my skin.

My eyes flutter shut and I drop the keys. "You have?"

"*Mmm.* I think part of me knew it was you when I saw your neck."

Holy shit. All I can do is stand there as he drags slow, open-mouthed kisses up and down my nape. "H-how?"

"I often sat behind you in class." There's a rough edge to his voice that sends a shiver down my spine, or maybe it's from his lips moving against the sensitive spot below my ear. "I lived for the days when you wore your hair up."

His teeth scrape lightly against the tendons of my throat, and the only reply I can verbalize is a broken moan.

"Fuck." His curse is savage, and he pulls away to scoop up the keys. "Which one?"

"Huh?"

"The *keys*, Torres. Which one?"

"Um, silver. Old looking."

He unlocks the door and all but shoves me inside. Our coats drop to the floor.

He backs me into the closed door and plucks the clips from my hair. His fingers tangle in the loose tresses as he nips my jaw. "I really only meant for us to talk."

I pull his mouth back to mine. "Later. I need this, too."

With a growl, he hikes up my dress with both hands and shoves down my thong. He hurries to undo his belt and open his pants, then freezes.

"Fuck, I don't have a condom—"

"I have an IUD."

I can't believe I just blurted that out, but his eyes glow with unabashed awe. That look sets me aflame, and I don't regret my admission.

"Yeah?" His voice is barely a whisper.

"Yeah. And I can show you my latest tests. It's been months since I was with anyone."

His Adam's apple bobs as he swallows, and I notice that his tie is loose, probably from me mangling it in the car.

"We'll compare results later," he says. "And me, too. Nearly a year."

Before I can wonder at that, his mouth crushes mine, and he grabs me by the thighs, hoisting me up. The door is hard against my back, and his chest pushes that goddamned battery pack into my sternum, but I don't give a shit. I reach between us, clasping his length and guiding him to my entrance. After all the foreplay in the car, I'm wet, but his dick is big. I wince when he pushes the head into me.

"Sorry." He halts, panting into my neck. "I swear I'll go down on you for hours later, I just need—"

"Me too," I whimper, cutting him off. "I need you inside me."

He lets out a harsh groan and sinks all the way in. My eyes roll back at the delicious fullness.

"Hang on." The command is issued in a hoarse whisper. "Gonna fuck you now."

Just the thought of it has me mewling, but I muster the wherewithal to clamp my thighs around his hips. And then all I can do is hold on for dear life as he slams into me. The angle is right, hitting just where I want it. My LEDs flicker on and off from his chest repeatedly bumping the power button. I bite my lip, muffling my moans while pleasure spirals through my limbs and my skin tingles.

And when he sucks on the sensitive place at the curve of my neck? I fucking unravel, quaking in his arms from a swift, blinding orgasm.

He fucks me through it, and mere moments later, his taut ass cheeks flex against my calves as he thrusts deep, locking our pelvises in place. He comes with a ragged groan.

Tension drains from his body. We're breathing hard and leaning all our weight against the door. When my brain finally comes back online, only two thoughts flit to the surface.

One: I just fucked Gideon Noble.

And two: It was *incredible*. The kind of effortlessly perfect sex I was searching for during my Hookup Era.

Why the hell did I have to find it with *Gideon Noble*, of all people?

Luckily, I don't have time to obsess further, because Noble exhales with a grunt and shifts his hips. His cock slips out of me, and I clench reflexively, feeling a trickle of wetness. God, why is that so hot? When he lets me down, it's nice to see we're both a little wobbly. I'm still regaining my balance when he drops a soft kiss on my forehead.

"Sorry." His voice is gruff and my heart sinks, because I know he's not apologizing for what we just did.

No, that "sorry" is for the past.

I'm not ready to dig into those memories yet, not until I can get a better grip on my emotional state. He's still wearing his tie, so I grab the end and tug him away from the door.

"Come on, Noble." I flash him a flirty smile. "Let's shower."

Chapter 6

GIDEON

I follow Torres in a daze. We're both quiet. I wish I knew what she was thinking. Fuck, I wish I knew what *I* was thinking. This is literally the shit I used to daydream about, but the reality of fucking Torres against her front door far exceeded anything my adolescent brain could've imagined, and I'm having a hard time catching up.

Her bathroom is typical of an old New York City apartment—tiny, with gray subway tiles and a black and white mosaic floor. She turns on the shower, and I help her unwind the lights from her torso. Then I finally remove my tie and unbutton my shirt while she strips off the red dress. I don't get a clear look at her body before she steps into the tub, just a flash of pale curves. I have the brief urge to leave now and avoid the coming conversation, but I don't. Second chance, right? I finish undressing and fold my clothes, then climb in after her.

She's washing her face, so I soap up quickly. The space is cramped, and we bump into each other as we bathe. Between the steam, the scent of lime bodywash, and the white noise of the spray, it's like being trapped in an intimate yet awkward cocoon. I've showered with sexual partners before, but this is *Valencia Torres*. Everything is different.

I sneak a glance as she runs the soapy loofah over her body. I want to follow the path it takes with my tongue, but the tub is already too small for the two of us, and I'm worried that if I try anything, we'll hurt ourselves. She passes me her face wash, then steps out.

A moment later, I hear her voice. "There's a towel hanging on the door for you. And I can give you something more comfortable to wear if you don't want to put your work clothes back on."

"Sure. Thanks." I wait in the tub, since there isn't room for both of us on the bath mat. After she leaves, I turn off the shower and step out to dry off. With the towel around my waist, I pick up my clothes and cross the hall to her bedroom. It's just big enough for a queen-size bed, a tall, narrow dresser, and a small nightstand stacked with books.

Torres is covered from armpit to knee in a towel as she stands on tiptoe to reach the top shelf of her tiny closet. When she hands me a yellow soccer jersey and a pair of men's running shorts, an uncomfortable thought crosses my mind.

"These aren't . . ."

When I trail off, she pauses with her hand on a jar of face lotion.

"Aren't what? They should fit you."

"They aren't . . ." I force myself to say the name. "Mulholland's?"

Because if they are, I'd sooner wear the lacy red thong I pulled off Torres earlier.

Her gaze flicks away from me. "No. They belonged to someone else."

I nod. I'm not jealous, per se. And it's not like I have an aversion to touching something of Mulholland's. It's more that I don't want to wear anything that will remind her of him.

When I unwrap the towel from my waist, I notice she's stealing glances from the corner of her eye.

I bite back a grin. "You can look."

She doesn't even try to deny what she was doing. It was difficult to get a good look in the shower, but the bedroom lamp casts a warm, bright glow, and there's nowhere to hide.

I leave off my boxers and take my time sliding the shorts up my legs and over my hips. Her lips part as she tracks the movement. I make sure to stretch and flex as I wriggle into the shirt. By the time I'm dressed, her cheeks are pink, and my dick is twitching in the borrowed shorts.

I shoot her a challenging smirk. "Your turn."

Eyebrows raised, her hands release the cloth tucked between her breasts, and the wet towel falls to the floor. She's naked and gorgeous, and I nearly swallow my tongue as I look my fill. Her dark locks are pinned up, and the delicate hairs around her face have started to curl from the shower steam. I take in her rosy nipples, the trimmed hair between her legs, her petite frame and dangerous curves. I'm hungry for her all over again.

But then she opens a drawer and covers herself with an oversize gray T-shirt and loose pajama shorts. The shirt features a quote from Supreme Court Justice Sonia Sotomayor that reads, "With fear for our democracy, I dissent." Somehow, this outfit is even more appealing than the tight red dress. She looks like the Valencia Torres I used to know—mission driven, focused, and *real*.

She collects the wet towels and shuffles out of the room in fuzzy purple slippers. "Come on. I'll make tea."

The kitchen is larger and newer than I'd expect for an apartment this small. There's even a dishwasher and washing machine. I tour the living room while the electric kettle heats water. Rows of crammed bookshelves line an entire wall, which is just so Torres. She was always reading when we were in school. But despite that, she never fit the stereotype of the shy, quiet bookworm. She'd been outspoken and friendly, full of ideas and ambition.

Except with me.

I drag a hand down my face as all the things I need to say to her crowd my thoughts. I wish I could call Ralph to help me get it all in order. To make sure I don't skip something or say it wrong.

Because part of me is already very attached to this conversation going right.

"Tea's ready." She hands me a mug, and I bring it to my nose to inhale.

"Chamomile?"

"It's a bit late for caffeine, but if you want something else, coffee or—"

"No, this is perfect."

She leads the way to a comfortable-looking yellow sofa. A Persian rug covers the hardwood floor, and between that and the exposed brick walls, the apartment feels cozy instead of cramped.

We sit side by side, blowing on our tea to cool it down. A massive gray cat with flattened ears appears out of nowhere and jumps onto the couch between us. When it settles against my hip, I slide my fingers through its fur and am rewarded with a purr like a rusty motor.

Valencia stifles a laugh with her hand.

I send her a puzzled look. "What's so funny?"

"Nothing." She says it quickly, then seems to change her mind about answering. "It's just . . . Archie isn't a fan of most people. Are you, boy?"

"Archie?"

"Short for Archimedes."

I scratch under the cat's chin and Archie's big yellow eyes roll back in bliss. "He seems to like me well enough."

She makes a noncommittal hum and sips her tea.

The silence that falls is taut with anticipation. We know what's coming but not how to get there.

Torres, as always, is braver than I am.

"You know," she begins, her tone thoughtful, "if someone had time-traveled from the future and told teenage me that I'd one day be sitting on my sofa with Gideon Noble, drinking herbal tea after he fucked my brains out, I probably would've slapped them in the face."

I want to focus on the "fucked my brains out" part, but force myself to stay on track. "You wouldn't have believed it?"

"Not in a million years." She narrows her eyes at me over her mug. "Don't tell me the thought of having sex with me ever crossed your mind."

"On the contrary. It crossed my mind *many* times. Sometimes multiple times a day."

She shoots me a look that says I'm full of shit. "You're lying."

"Have you seen yourself?"

Her mouth drops open. "What is this revisionist history? You are the same person who said my eyebrows looked like turds. You told everyone I didn't wash my hair. And you called me *Smellencia* for *two years*."

Remorse is like a knife in my chest. It kills me that this is what she remembers about me. I hold her gaze and say, as sincerely as possible, "I know. And I'm sorry. I was an asshole."

"Exactly." Her voice is high with indignation. "So don't you dare try to claim you secretly thought I was pretty or some bullshit."

I sit up straight, a tough feat on this sofa. "Do you remember the Christmas dance in eighth grade?"

She rolls her eyes. "How could I forget? That was the night I finally learned to use a flat iron and asked my mom to tweeze my eyebrows. And suddenly, thanks to my *Princess Diaries* makeover, all the boys who'd teased me since sixth grade fell over themselves to ask me to dance." She raises those brows at me now, as if to emphasize their elegantly angled arches.

I pitch my voice low to contrast her flippant tone. "You wore an emerald green dress. Velvet. I know, because I bumped into you by the snack table and touched your sleeve. Your hair was pulled back in a bun, but you had these pieces falling down, here"—I graze a fingertip from her temple to her chin—"and here." I repeat the touch on the other side of her face.

She's quiet for a moment, studying me with her dark, piercing gaze. "*You* didn't ask me to dance."

"I know."

I wish to God that I had. Maybe things would've turned out differently between us.

"Why—" She breaks off and shakes her head.

"Go ahead. You can ask." Answering her questions is the least I can do.

A line forms between her brows, and old hurt lingers in her eyes. "Why didn't you ask me? And why did you tease me so much before that? And then . . . why did you stop? In high school, you acted like I didn't exist. Was it because of the dance?"

I lean back and wrap my hands around the warm mug. "It's . . . a lot more complicated than that."

"So tell me." There's the faintest note of pleading in her voice, so I take a deep breath and bring forward those old, shameful feelings.

"From the beginning, you were so smart, and so focused, it kind of drove me nuts. I was consumed with a mix of admiration and jealousy. There were times I thought you had to be cheating, because how could anyone be so fucking brilliant? But I was attracted to you, too, and I didn't know how to deal with any of it except to try to distract you."

"So you annoyed me because you wanted attention. How original." Her glare is unimpressed. "It didn't occur to you that you could just be my *friend*?"

"I—no."

"Why the fuck not?" She sounds incredulous, and I can't blame her.

I deflate, because this part is even harder to admit. It feels disloyal, even though he's gone, even though he was *wrong*. But I owe this to her, so I say, "Because . . . because of my dad."

Her brow furrows, and something like compassion tinges her expression. "I remember he was hard on you. About grades."

I'm surprised she knows that, but then again, we were in school together for seven years. There are a lot of things we know about each other.

I scratch the back of my neck. "He, um, basically instilled in me a very entitled mindset."

"You don't say." Her tone is mildly teasing, and it makes it easier to go on.

"He told me I should be at the top of our class, and if I wasn't, it was simultaneously because I wasn't trying hard enough and other people were taking what was mine." I rub my forehead, then blurt out the rest. "He especially didn't like that a girl was besting me."

She rolls her eyes. "I'm sure the double *R* in my last name didn't help."

I wince, because she's not wrong. "He might've made some comments about diversity admissions."

At that, she makes a disgusted sound. "Noble, look at me. If it weren't for my name, no one would guess I was Puerto Rican. And yes, I got *some* financial assistance for tuition, but my parents were doctors, and I earned my grades by working my ass off."

"I know all that. It was stupid, and by the time I realized why my dad had it out for you, by the time I realized he was the reason why I thought it was okay to tease you, why I felt entitled to your attention, why I was jealous of your grades . . . it was too late. We were never going to be friends."

Her brow scrunches. "Okay, but you went from daily teasing—which, honestly, I'd gotten used to—to acting like I was invisible. That was a mindfuck in a different way."

My heart sinks. "I'm sorry. I never even considered that would bother you."

"Then why'd you do it?"

"I heard my dad say some things that were, well, eye opening. And I started rethinking everything."

I'd been fifteen when I overheard my dad going on a tirade about immigration. Never mind that my own mother, his *wife*, was a French model who'd overstayed her visa when she was in her twenties, and that was how she'd met my father in New York. The hypocrisy had shocked me, although it shouldn't have. Maybe I'd been too focused on trying to gain his approval to connect the dots sooner. He'd always been prone to mood swings, and nothing I did was ever good enough. And this was around the time I'd started to accept that I was also attracted to guys, and fear over what my father would say if he found out contributed to my drawing inward in high school.

Now I take pro bono immigration cases on the side, working within the framework of a cruel and broken system, as well as donating through my family's foundation. But it still doesn't feel like enough to outweigh the damage Malcolm Noble did with his money, money that's now mine to do with as I please because I didn't rock the boat while he was alive.

Yes, I'm unpacking all this with Ralph. And no, I'm nowhere near finished processing everything. But I don't want Torres doing any more emotional labor on my behalf, so I only say, "I figured the best thing I could do was leave you alone."

She gives me an arch look. "I think the best thing you could've done was *apologize*."

I cringe. "Unfortunately, that didn't occur to me. So I just didn't say . . . anything."

"Until graduation."

I run a hand down my face. "I was hoping you'd forgotten about that."

"How could I?" Her eyes spark with irritation. "You tormented me and then ignored me, and suddenly you come up after the ceremony to shake my hand and wish me—and I quote—'the best of luck in all your endeavors.'"

I can't help but laugh at her derisive imitation of my voice. "God, I was such a tool. I can't believe I said that."

"I spent *months* trying to figure out what that was supposed to mean."

"I swear I wasn't trying to be cryptic."

"What *were* you doing?"

I rub the back of my neck. "I was aiming for polite. And brief. You were with Mulholland by that point, and I didn't want him to see me talking to you."

"Worried he was going to kick your ass?" I expect her to smirk, but her lips are pressed into a humorless line.

"Absolutely. After he had that growth spurt junior year, nobody messed with him."

Her eyes narrow. "You really just wanted to wish me luck?"

"I really did. You worked hard, earned the top spot, and . . . I wanted you to do well. You know, in life."

She releases an annoyed huff. "So basic. Would you have written 'have a nice life' in my yearbook, if I'd asked you to sign it?"

"I—yeah, probably. Because other people would've seen it."

"Ah." A knowing look crosses her features. "What would you have written if it were private?"

I blow out a breath. "I—"

"Wait, don't tell me." She opens a drawer in the antique wooden coffee table and pulls out a pen and a spiral notebook made from recycled paper. "Write it down."

"Write what down?"

"What you would've written in my yearbook if no one else could see it."

Adrenaline floods my body. "Right now?"

"Yes. You owe me this."

"Oh, my God." I accept the paper and pen, feeling extremely silly.

And then I take a moment to get my head on straight.

Ralph would tell me there's nothing wrong with looking silly. That my father is gone, and even if he weren't, I don't need to live up to his definition of masculinity. That being vulnerable and having feelings doesn't make you weak. That rejection and failure aren't death sentences.

I glance at Valencia, who's sipping her tea and scratching her cat's odd folded ears.

Second chance, I think.

Then I click open the pen and begin to write.

Chapter 7

GIDEON

Dear Torres,

I'm sorry. I could write those words on every line in this notebook, and it still wouldn't be enough. I was an insufferable little shit, and I made you the target of my insecurities for stupid and childish reasons that had nothing to do with you.

The truth is, you're the most beautiful woman I've ever seen, and the smartest person I've ever known. I wish I'd had the courage to tell you that before, and the guts to apologize sooner.

I mean this with all sincerity: Have a nice
life. No one deserves it more.
Love,
Gideon

I stare down at the words I've written. They flowed out of
me, like water bursting through a dam, but as I imagine Torres
reading them, panic grips me in a vise and my face flames.

No. Fuck vulnerability. This is too raw. She can't see
this. She—

Rips the notebook out of my hand.

I lunge for it, and Torres dances out of the way, laughing.
But as she reads, her gleeful smile fades.

"There. Are you happy?" I feel exposed, and I can't help
snapping at her. God, I'm so fucked up. I reach for my cold tea
and gulp it down, wishing it were whiskey.

She's still staring at the paper, but I know she's finished.
What is she thinking? Is she going to laugh at me? Kick me
out? Accuse me of lying again?

Once upon a time, I would've sneered at her and turned
the whole thing into a joke. Anything to avoid being viewed as
weak. That insecure kid still lives inside me, and his protective
impulses persist, even though I've matured enough not to
act on them.

"You have to learn to sit with discomfort," Ralph's always telling me. "It won't kill you."

Maybe my body won't die from spilling my feelings to this woman, but my ego is kicking and screaming like it's being dragged to the gallows.

I wait, every muscle tense, my gaze trained on her face. What is taking her so fucking long?

"Gideon." She whispers my first name, and I jolt. I can't recall the last time I heard her use it on its own without full-naming me like you do with people you knew in school. When her eyes lift, they're shiny. "Thank you."

The air leaves my lungs in a rush, and my voice comes out harsh. "Torres, don't. For God's sake, don't thank me."

But she rounds the coffee table to kneel beside me on the sofa cushions. The cat is gone, having leaped up when Torres grabbed the notebook, which she now tosses aside.

"I needed that." She speaks softly, winding her arms around my neck. Her chest presses against mine as she hugs me. "I needed to know it wasn't me."

I hesitate for just a second, then wrap myself around her, inhaling her scent as I close my eyes. "It was never your fault."

"I know. I told myself that, but . . . it helps to hear it."

"I really am sorry."

"It's in the past." She rests her head on my shoulder, and something within me, a tension I've been carrying for what feels like forever, eases slightly.

Maybe I don't deserve her grace. But I soak it in all the same.

After a moment, she leans back. "You still have beautiful handwriting."

"You remember my handwriting?"

A soft smile plays on her lips. "I remember a lot about you."

She says it like she's not only referencing the bad shit. I lean my head toward her. "It only took fourteen years, but I finally got to dance with you at a Christmas party."

Her eyes warm. "I'm glad we did. Tonight was nice."

"Nice?" I can't help but smirk. "You call what we did against your door *nice*?"

"Not *that*. That was . . ." She sounds flustered as she stops to blow out a breath. "That was way more than nice. At the club, I mean. Fern left early, and even though I know her friends, it wasn't the same. And since I'm skipping Christmas this year, it was good to have company."

My brow furrows. "Why are you skipping Christmas? Not a fan?"

"No, I love Christmas. It's my favorite time of year."

"Then why?"

She picks up her mug and takes a small sip. "I'm not sure if you heard, but my parents passed away three years ago."

I'm sure my shock is evident on my face, and without planning to, I clutch her free hand. "Oh, shit. I had no idea. Both of them?"

She nods. Her gaze falls to her lap, but her fingers squeeze mine. "Car accident. Coming back from our beach house in Jersey."

"Torres, I . . . That's terrible. I'm so sorry. That must have been really hard." There are no appropriate words for this level of tragedy. The hole that has lived inside me since my father's death echoes, as if resonating with the chasm that must live within her.

"Thanks." She gives a little shrug, but I see the pain mirrored in her eyes. "It *was* hard. But I wasn't alone. I had Everett, and Fern, and their parents. Heather and Patrick already felt like family, and they were going to be my in-laws. I leaned on them a lot."

I can guess where this is going. "But now that you and Mulholland . . ."

"Right. Even though we're not together anymore, his mom still wants me to do all the holiday stuff with them."

"Do you want to?"

"I don't particularly want to be alone, but I don't want them to feel obligated to include me, you know?"

I'm desperate to know the details of her breakup, but it's not my place to ask.

"Are you going there Christmas Day?"

"No, I've got other plans."

She doesn't elaborate, but since she's shared something personal, I feel like I should reciprocate.

"This is the first Christmas without my father, and my mom is in France. She's not coming back until the twenty-fourth. Christmas was always a big deal in our home, so this is . . . different."

"What would you be doing if everything were the way it used to be?"

I twine my fingers with hers as I consider the question. "Well, today is December thirteenth, which means my mother would have already enlisted my help in putting up the Christmas tree a couple weeks ago. Not decorating it, mind you. She plans her designs months in advance, but actually standing the tree in the holder? That's my job."

Torres smiles, as I hoped she would. "It's good to have a career option if finance doesn't work out."

"Hey, it's harder than you'd think, especially if you're trying to meet Andrea Noble's exacting standards."

"Oh, I believe you. If you recall, I was at your thirteenth birthday party."

I groan. "God, that was over the top, even for me."

"Only if you classify hiring the entire cast of *Rock of Ages* to perform in your apartment as 'over the top.'"

"Look, it wasn't my idea. I don't even like jukebox musicals."

"Ay, pobrecito." She pouts mockingly, and I want to kiss her so fucking bad.

"What about you? Were you allowed to do more than put the tree in the holder?" It's an obvious bid to steer the topic away from my family, but she accepts the shift.

"Not only allowed, but encouraged." She cuddles against my side, and I put my arm around her. The move feels natural, even though we've never done anything like this before. "My family had a huge collection of ornaments. My mom labeled all of them, noting when and where we got them."

"Do you still have those?"

She nods, but her smile turns sad. "They're in storage. I haven't been able to bring myself to take them out."

I stroke her arm. Giving comfort doesn't come easily for me, but with Torres, I want to try. "What other traditions did you have?"

Her eyes take on a dreamy quality, as if she's sifting through fond memories. "The usual stuff. Baking cookies, ice-skating, seeing the tree at Rockefeller Center, and the train show at the Botanical Garden."

"You should still do all that," I tell her, but she shakes her head.

"After my parents died, I at least had Everett and his family to celebrate with. But this year? I'd rather skip all of it than do it alone."

An idea comes to me, and even though I'm scared to voice it, I do anyway. "What if we did those things together?"

Only about one second passes before she glances up at me, and it's the longest second of my life. The clench in my gut eases when I see the hope shining in her eyes.

"You'd do that?" she whispers.

"You love Christmas." I keep my tone light, aiming to mask how serious this suddenly feels. "You should get to enjoy what you love."

She chews the corner of her lower lip and watches my face carefully. "It won't be difficult for you? Because of your own . . . loss?"

I shake my head. "Maybe it's not cool to admit, but I love Christmas, too. The lights, the music, gingerbread and eggnog—I'm a sucker for all that shit. And it'll be good for me to do something other than work, overexercise, and dwell on my emotionally fucked-up childhood."

Her face lights up, as if she's more excited by the prospect of helping me than she is by partaking in yuletide cheer. "Let's make a list. Counting today, there are twelve days until Christmas Eve. That's when your mom arrives, right?"

"Right."

"Let's do something every day until then. And maybe we can spice things up a little, too."

"What do you have in mind?"

She taps the end of the pen against her lips as she thinks. "For example, on one day we can go to the Union Square Holiday Market for hot chocolate."

I pull a face. "It'll be packed."

"We don't have to stay long. And after that we can, I don't know, watch porn."

Her matter-of-fact tone has me choking on air. "Excuse me?"

"Try to keep up, Noble. As far as hookups go, I'd say this one was pretty successful, wouldn't you? And after the year we've both had, we deserve to deck the halls a little."

"In more ways than one." I smirk, even though the term *hookup* gives me a weird pang.

"Exactly. So if we're making a list of Christmas activities, why not make a list of sexual ones, too?"

Twelve nights of sex with Valencia Torres? This is a dream come true. "Count me in."

"Great." She flashes me a brilliant smile. "Today is Day 1. Could we call the club a Christmas party?"

"Maybe SantaCon."

"But that's tomorrow."

"So? There were people dressed as Santa, and this means we can avoid the madness of *actual* SantaCon."

"Good call." She writes in the notebook, then chews lightly on the end of the pen. "What should we write in the sex column for today?"

My grin is devilish. "Exhibitionism."

I expect her to look embarrassed, but she cackles with something like glee. "I can't believe we felt each other up in front of your friends."

"Rodrigo and Bailey have felt each other up plenty of times in front of me. It was my turn." My work husband is going to have a lot of questions about tonight, but that's a problem for tomorrow.

The pen hovers near her mouth again, and I watch it like a hawk.

"Sledding? Nah, there's no snow in the forecast."

"Christmas movies," I say absently. "Can you tap your lip again with the—*mmm*, just like that. Fuck, why is that so hot?"

With a coy smile, she runs the pen's clicker around the outline of her lips. "Are you harboring a latent teacher or librarian fantasy? Ooh, I should add role-play to the list." She writes it down, then brings the pen back to her mouth, slowly darting her tongue out to lick it.

I grab the pen and toss it aside, replacing it with my thumb. When I nudge her mouth open, her lips purse around the tip, and she teases the edge of my nail with her tongue.

"You are so fucking sexy I can't stand it." My voice is like gravel, and in response, her eyes go molten. She grabs the collar of my borrowed shirt, pulling me on top of her until I'm pressing her into the couch cushions.

The fire that flared between us when we entered the apartment is back in full force.

I kiss her, stroking deep into her mouth with my tongue. She surprises me by catching my bottom lip between her teeth.

"This fucking mouth." Her voice is hoarse as she soothes my lip with her tongue. "This stubborn, bratty, *luscious* fucking mouth."

Electricity sizzles through my veins. "In about thirty seconds, you're going to see what else this mouth can do." I trail kisses down her neck, stopping to suck, to nip, to lick.

"Is that so?" She tilts her head back to give me better access.

"You forgot already?" I push up to look her in the eye. "I promised to go down on you for hours."

"Oh, God." Her lashes flutter, and she strokes her thumb over my lower lip. "You'd better get started, then."

It doesn't take hours. Within five minutes of me lapping at her clit and pulsing my fingers inside her, she's pulling my hair and begging me to let her come. I do, savoring her soft little whimpers as she bucks against my face. After she calms, I'm down to keep going, but she turns the tables on me and kneels on the floor between my feet.

Heaven. Her mouth on my cock is absolute heaven. Her lips, her tongue, the inside of her cheek, the slight drag of her teeth on my shaft—each sensation sends shivers along my spine. And her eyes, looking up at me from my lap, are the sexiest thing I've ever seen.

It's quick and perfect, and after I've caught my breath, I drag her up my body to kiss her mouth. We taste like each other's releases, and it's another jolt of unexpected intimacy.

She pulls away before I'm ready and wriggles back into her underwear and pajama bottoms. "Don't think I'm not banking the rest of those hours you owe me. Now, what else should we add to our list?"

"How can you think about lists after what we just did?" My heart is still racing, and the air saws in and out of my lungs. I barely muster the energy to slip my dick back into the borrowed shorts.

She's already scribbling away. "You know how goal oriented I am."

"That's true." I reach for her tea, which is still half full, and drain the mug.

"I'll make more." She starts to get up, but I wave her off.

"I've got it. You work on the list."

While I'm perusing her selection of teas, the cat strolls into the kitchen and winds around my bare ankles. I hold two boxes out to him, and he bumps his head against the one in my left hand. Decaf jasmine green tea it is.

With the cat at my heels, I carry our tea back to the living room.

At the look of alarm on Torres's face, I freeze. "What's wrong?"

Her eyes flick over me, from the mugs to the cat rubbing against my legs, and she shakes her head quickly. "Nothing. I was just thinking."

"About the list?"

"Um, yeah."

I set the mugs on the coffee table and sit next to her. "What else have you written down?"

"Uh, the window displays on Fifth Avenue."

"How unexpectedly capitalist of you."

"Shush. Ice-skating at Wollman Rink."

"Are we tourists?"

"It's iconic for a reason." She grabs a crocheted throw blanket from the back of the sofa and tucks it over our laps. "Anything you want to add?"

Before I can think twice, I say, "The Rockettes."

She shoots me a wary look. "Is this your way of suggesting an orgy?"

That pulls a surprised laugh from me. "No, but also . . . maybe? I mean the Radio City Christmas Spectacular. I used to go with my parents when I was a kid. It just wasn't Christmas without that."

Her expression softens, and she writes it down.

We go back and forth, adding items in both categories, when Torres introduces a new rule.

"If we both have it, we both have to do it."

"Have what?"

"The body part. I'm not letting you make a list of things you only do to me. These are equal opportunity sexcapades, buddy."

I glance at what I've just written and groan.

"Let me see that." For the second time tonight, she snatches the notebook from me. This time, she lets out a chortle. *"Butt plugs?"*

"We can cross it out—"

"Oh, no, you don't. Consider this chiseled in stone. Butt plugs all around!"

I drag a hand down my face and sigh.

By the time Valencia and Gideon's Naughty and Nice List is complete, it's three in the morning. We're leaning against each other on the sofa, cuddled under a chunky crocheted blanket, when she lets loose a jaw-cracking yawn.

"I'm going to head home before I fall asleep," I say through my own yawn, even though I want nothing more than to curl up with her all night. "See you tomorrow?"

"Yes, for tree decorating and"—she consults the list—"tickling."

"It's a date." I heave myself off the sofa.

At first, I indulged the idea of the list because I wanted to cheer her up. But I'm glad to have a valid excuse to see her again. Every day until Christmas Eve, according to her rules.

I don't deserve a minute of her time, not after the way I treated her when we were younger. But she deserves to not be alone for Christmas. And I'm just enough of a bastard to use that to my advantage. If all I get are twelve days, I'm going to make the most of them.

The truth is? I don't want to be alone, either.

And more than that, I want to be *not alone* with Valencia Torres.

Once I'm back in my own clothes, she walks me to the door. Before she shuts it, she sends me a small, secret smile. "Good night . . . Gideon."

The corner of my mouth ticks up. "Good night, Valencia."

I whistle "Have Yourself a Merry Little Christmas" as I jog down the stairs and emerge into the night.

Chapter 8

Valencia

Day 2: Tickling & Tree Decorating

Gideon and I exchanged numbers, and through text messages, we decide that I'll get the tree and dinner, and he'll bring decorations and "additional accessories." I assume the latter refers to tickling, and I spend all day Saturday obsessing over what he could possibly be buying. I didn't think about it while we were making the list, but some of the prompts involve items I certainly don't have on hand.

Like, Lord help me, *nipple clamps*.

At one minute to six, our scheduled meeting time, the intercom buzzes. The sound sends Archie tearing out of the room to hide in the hall closet. I press the button to let Gideon into the building and try to wipe the pleased smile off my face.

What can I say? I appreciate punctuality.

I open the front door as he reaches the landing. He's wearing a gray wool coat unbuttoned over a steel blue sweater and dark slacks. His hair is styled like it was last night before I ran my hands through it, and my fingers itch to ruffle those wheat-colored waves again.

His eyes light up when he sees me. "Hi."

I step aside to let him in. "Welcome back."

As he passes me, I'm struck once again by how big he is, and my mouth goes dry. He's tall, but lean, and it wasn't until I saw him completely naked in my bedroom that I was able to fully appreciate his broad shoulders, trim hips, and the sculpted body hidden by his perfectly tailored clothes.

I don't miss the way his gaze drifts toward the door as I shut it, and I'd bet money he's also remembering what we did there last night.

Ignoring the way my pulse throbs at the memory, I gesture him onward. "Dinner's on the kitchen counter. And the tree's on the table, since Archie never jumps on there."

I hang up Gideon's coat, which probably cost twenty times more than mine. It carries the scent of his cologne, and I resist the urge to bury my face in it. He slides his shoes into an empty spot on the shoe rack, then hands me one of the canvas bags he's carrying. I open it and find a collection of ornaments shaped like books. They feature banned novels written by female authors, and it takes me a moment to realize we read all of these in high school together.

A business card states that they were made from recycled materials, and I know in my gut that he looked up the EPA's guidance on having a green holiday. His thoughtfulness overwhelms me, but when I go into the kitchen to thank him, he brushes me off, bustling around as if he's been here a hundred times instead of once.

That's fine, since I don't really know what to say anyway. This is a twelve-day holiday hookup—no more, no less. Come Christmas morning, I'll be volunteering at a local food kitchen. I didn't tell Gideon, in case he felt obligated to include me in his plans with his mom or offered to come with me. The rest of the year will be spent packing, and in January I'll find a new apartment and go back to living and breathing my job, which won't leave any room for fun and games with my former nemesis.

I say "former" because while Gideon might have been a giant pain in the ass when we were kids, he's now incredibly easy to be around. Honestly, it's unnerving. And after everything he shared last night, I have a vulnerability hangover. I'm satisfied with his explanation—and let's face it, kids can be really mean to each other, even without their parents sowing seeds of hate—but I don't know how to reconcile the Gideon I remember with who he is now.

The best thing I can do is stick to the activities on our list, engage in some great sex with a hot guy, and once Christmas is over, go back to my regularly scheduled life.

I ordered dim sum, and he sets the table while I put on Christmas music. We eat next to the two-foot-tall potted spruce I picked up this afternoon, and which my landlord agreed to add to the plants in front of the building.

"What did you do today?" I ask, before devouring a soup dumpling.

He swallows a bite of noodles. "Rodrigo and I went on a shopping spree."

I raise my eyebrows. "Oh?"

"You know that high-end sex store on Seventh Avenue?"

"Yeah, it's been there forever." My eyes widen as I realize what he's implying. "Wait, Rodrigo helped you buy sex toys for *us*?"

His full lips tremble like he's trying not to laugh. "That's what work husbands are for."

"No, work husbands are for keeping you company at lunch, not sex-toy shopping!"

"We have a list, and I needed his expert opinion."

"You told him about our list? Did he think it was weird?"

Gideon rolls his eyes. "Let's just say he was *very* supportive."

I don't ask for further details. "What did you buy?"

His grin is wicked. "You'll see."

My face flushes, and I swallow hard. "Well, I'll pay you back. Just send me the receipt."

That ruins the moment, and Gideon makes a disgusted sound in the back of his throat. "You absolutely will not."

"But—"

"*No*, Valencia."

It's the usage of my first name that halts me. The way his deep voice caresses all four syllables sends a thrum through my body.

Everett used to call me "V" most of the time, and I didn't mind it. Or, at least, I got used to it. But I like my name.

And I *really* like how Gideon says it.

"Fine. Be that way." I make my tone snippy to disguise my real reaction.

The look he gives me is exasperated and fond, all at the same time.

After dinner, Gideon helps clean up. We sing along to Nat King Cole, Mariah Carey, and Michael Bublé while we deck the halls with pine boughs and strings of energy-efficient LED lights. I'm still not ready to dig out my parents' ornaments, so I appreciate that Gideon thought to buy me new ones, even if he won't let me pay him back for those, either. He also picked up a couple of quilted stockings made from repurposed fabric. For me and Archie, he says.

I moved into this apartment with Everett when I was twenty-two. He took all his stuff when he left and I've made it my own, but with Gideon here, the space feels different in a way I can't explain. Gideon has an innate confidence in his own skin that seems to extend to the area around him, as if the force of his personality conforms the environment to his will.

Archie must feel it, too. He usually hides when someone else is around, and he used to actively hiss at Everett. But with Gideon, Archie rubs right up against him, shedding gray fur all over Gideon's expensive black trousers.

Gideon doesn't seem to mind, though. He scratches Archie's head and murmurs baby talk to him in what sounds suspiciously like French.

I really need Gideon to pick his nose or something. Nothing egregious, just something unpleasant enough to make him a little less irresistible.

We're having such a nice time, I almost forget about our other activity, but Gideon has one more gift for me.

"What's this?" I ask, taking the long package wrapped delicately in tissue paper. It barely weighs anything.

"Open it." His green eyes sparkle like something from a dragon's hoard, reflecting the twinkling lights all around us.

Oh, boy. I know exactly what this is.

I carefully unfold the layers of paper, revealing a fluffy black ostrich feather attached to a slim metal rod.

Since I'm on the verge of making a terrible pun about "tickling my fancy," I say blandly, "Well, come on, then."

In the bedroom, I set the feather on top of the books stacked on my bedside table. My heartbeat pounds in my throat like a snare. Last night, I was fueled by the illicit thrill of fucking a guy who used to hate me. But now? I have no idea how to begin.

I turn to face him and catch his eyes darting over to the bed. Remembering how he asked if the clothes I gave him last night had belonged to Everett, I blurt out, "It's a new mattress." My face flames, but I need him to know that this is not the same bed I had sex with Everett Mulholland on.

Gideon just nods, but his jaw is tight, and he looks as jittery as I feel.

So I do what anyone would do in this situation: I rip my sweater over my head and throw it on the floor.

Sure enough, Gideon's lips part as his gaze fixes on my chest, because the only thing I have on under the sweater is a red lace bralette.

His eyes flick back to mine and he raises a brow. "Does this mean you're volunteering to go first?"

Shit, I hadn't thought of that, but I give a brave nod. "Yes. I volunteer as tribute."

Gideon grins and pulls off his own sweater, followed by his undershirt. I shove down my leggings and kick them off before climbing onto the bed in nothing but my bra and matching panties. The heat in Gideon's eyes intensifies as he picks up the feather.

I lie on my back with my arms and legs straight. Goosebumps break out over my skin. I stare at the ceiling and drag in a deep, calming breath.

In the periphery, I'm aware of Gideon moving to the foot of the bed.

"I'm going to start with your feet. Do you consent?"

I let out a shaky breath. "Go ahead."

"All right. Here it comes."

He steps closer, and from the corner of my eye, I see his arm move. A second later, the feather flicks over the arch of my left foot in the barest of touches.

I react like he's zapped me with a taser.

My heel nearly catches Gideon in the face. He jerks backward as I vault off the bed like Simone Biles going for another gold medal. I make a beeline for the bathroom, giggling the whole way.

When I come back from peeing, I find Gideon sitting on the edge of the bed with Archie. Gideon looks up when I enter the room, a sheepish smile on his face.

"I don't suppose you want to try that again?"

I shake my head vehemently. "No way."

His shoulders slump in relief. "Thank God. You almost broke my nose."

"Sorry. But I know how to make it up to you."

His brows lift. "Oh, yeah?"

I raise the feather and wave it in the air. "Your turn."

With a resigned sigh, he lies down on the bed, which Archie takes as his cue to depart. While I was gone, Gideon removed his socks. All he's wearing are his pants, which are now covered in cat fur. I make a mental note to use a lint roller on them before he leaves.

Kneeling on the mattress beside him, I drag the fluffy ends of the feather along his abdomen, wishing it was my mouth trailing kisses over his flushed skin. I roll the rod between my fingers, making the feather swish side to side as I trace the lines and contours of his muscles. I'm so focused on the enticing vee at his hips that it takes me longer than it should to realize he's practically shaking from the effort of holding still. His fists are white-knuckled where they grip the quilt, and when I look at his face, his lips are pressed into a stoic line.

"Forget it." I toss the feather aside. "I think we should just fuck."

The words are barely out of my mouth before he pins me to the bed and kisses me senseless. His ardor ignites my own, and I grapple with the fastenings on his pants. We're both on edge, maybe from the tickling, maybe from the unexpectedly pleasant evening. That could just be me. Either way, we tear the rest of each other's clothes off, and before I know it, he's got my knees pushed up and his face between my thighs. He mutters something about paying down his debt, but I'm gasping too much to respond.

When I'm boneless and quivering from a mind-blowing orgasm, he moves up to curl around my side. Hooking his elbow under my knee, he splays me open and slides into me in one continuous thrust. The penetration pulls a long groan from my throat that somehow ends with his name. He murmurs something unintelligible into my neck and then he sets a pace that makes it impossible for me to think. At some point, he grabs the feather and trails it down my torso, a move that causes me to buck my hips wildly and clench my inner walls. He grits out, "Fucking worth it," and slams into me harder.

He hits the right spot, over and over, and I climax again. After a few more hard pumps, he pulls out, jerking his cock and groaning until he comes on my pussy in a warm splash.

His head drops onto my chest and neither of us moves for a full minute. I'm achingly aware of his heart hammering against my ribs as aftershocks zing through me.

Gideon is scary good at this. How the fuck am I supposed to get through ten more days?

Finally, he moves, but not to get up. Instead, he drags the feather between my legs, soaking the silky plume with our combined juices. Then he lifts it up to show it to me.

It's one of the hottest things I've ever seen.

And I very much need to bring us back to earth.

"Okay," I say, struggling to find my voice. "On a scale of one to five: tickling."

He huffs out a breathless laugh that stirs my hair. "The actual tickling part? One-point-five. *Maybe* two. The way we absolutely ruined that feather?" He tilts his head to send me an indulgent look. "Five stars."

That look does something to me, so I grab a clip from the nightstand and focus on twisting my hair up into a bun. "I'd have to say the same about tickling. I nearly peed myself."

His tone is amused. "And we don't even have that on our list."

"Yeah, that's not changing. My adventurous side has its limits."

Like butt plugs, I think, and a new shiver of anticipation runs up my spine.

"And the Christmas activity?" I ask, changing the subject. "Scale of one to five: tree decorating."

He's quiet for a moment, staring at the ceiling. "Five stars," he says softly, and doesn't offer any more commentary.

Finally, I say, "Me too," and shift to get off the bed.

We take turns cleaning up in the bathroom, and while Gideon's in there, I use the lint roller on his pants. As Gideon is putting on his shoes, Archie trots out of the hall closet as if he also wants to say goodbye. I pick up my cat to keep my hands occupied. Otherwise, I might rip Gideon's fancy coat right back off him. My pulse races at the thought, but I only offer a friendly smile when he steps closer.

"See you tomorrow?" I say it like a question, giving him an out in case he doesn't want to continue this thing we've started. But all he does is nod and scratch Archie under the chin.

"Tomorrow." And then, with a mischievous grin, Gideon tickles my neck. I'm giggling when he says, "Good night, Valencia," and opens the door.

I whisper back, "Good night, Gideon," and close it behind him.

I take a deep breath, and my whole body goes hot as I visualize tomorrow's activity.

Nipple clamps.

Chapter 9

Valencia

Day 3: Nipple Clamps & Ice-Skating

Throughout my childhood, I went ice-skating with my parents every December, often right here at the historic Wollman Rink in Central Park. So I'd consider myself a competent skater. At the very least, I can circle a rink without falling.

Gideon, however, is disgustingly good.

As he does yet *another* spin, I glare at him.

"You've had lessons." I say it like I'm accusing him of murder. But when I plant my hands on my hips, I stumble and have to shoot my arms out for balance.

He only shrugs and skates backward at my side, his hands clasped behind him. "My mom once dreamed of her son being an Olympic athlete. Alas, I was forced to disappoint her."

"Just a lowly lawyer," I joke. "How embarrassing."

He smirks. "Precisely."

But when I wobble again, he takes my hand and doesn't let go until it's time to leave.

I'd be fine taking the subway from the park to Gideon's apartment, but after he notices me wincing when I put my boots on, he insists on hailing a taxi. While we're in the car, he places an order at a French bistro so we won't have to wait long for lunch to arrive.

Gideon lives in a high-rise in Chelsea overlooking the Hudson River. He nods to the uniformed doorman when we enter, and we ride the elevator to one of the topmost floors.

His apartment is lavish, with floor-to-ceiling windows, a fireplace in the living room, and expensive-looking leather and chrome furniture. The space was clearly decorated by a professional—or, perhaps, by his mother—but the colorful rugs covering the hardwood floors prevent it from feeling cold and impersonal.

While he's in the bathroom, I peruse his bookshelf. There are big hardcovers about art and architecture, and a collection of titles about New York City history. I examine the street photography lining the walls, and I'm suddenly hit with a memory of a teenage Gideon Noble with a camera slung around his neck. His hair was blonder, his body leaner, and—I'd forgotten this—his ears were pierced, the small diamond studs softening the sharp beauty of his face.

"You were on the yearbook committee," I say when he comes back into the living room.

"I was one of the photographers."

"Are any of these yours?" I gesture to the walls.

He nods, coming over to join me. "These." He points to a row of three smaller photos. They're in black and white, and the quality is a little grainy, but each shows a crowd of people somewhere in New York. Most are blurred out, faces down, hurrying about their lives. But in the center of each photo, still and crisply in focus, is a single person looking up. Not at the camera. Not at their phones. It's unclear what caught their attention, only that, in each of these instances, someone stopped long enough to be captured by the camera. Or, more accurately, by Gideon's eye.

I feel strangely jealous of these three random people who stood out to him in a crowd.

Next to me, Gideon speaks, unprompted. "I like art that makes you feel something without telling you what to feel."

I exhale, unsure how to reply. Because the truth is, I'm feeling something right now, and it's not entirely welcome.

Swallowing it down, I cast about for something that doesn't require any feeling at all. My eyes settle on his sleek leather couch, and I murmur, "Archie would absolutely demolish that sofa."

Gideon winces. "I can only imagine."

His phone buzzes, notifying us that our food is on the way up, and I'm grateful for the distraction.

We sit at his dining table, where I read aloud an article about nipple clamps for beginners. The tone of the piece is cheeky, and we joke and send flirtatious looks at each other while we eat.

I'm munching on deliciously salty pommes frites when a thought occurs to me.

"Communication," I say.

His brows furrow in confusion as he chews, so I explain.

"Regardless of best practices, communication is going to be key with some of these prompts. Especially since I'm a Scorpio and you're a Capricorn."

He blinks. "Excuse me, who are you and what have you done with Valencia Torres?"

I throw a fry at him. "Shut up."

"No, I'm serious. You're the last person I'd expect to bring up zodiac signs. Didn't you once say horoscopes are, and I quote, 'New Age pseudointellectual bullshit'?"

"That was in seventh grade! And Eva Parker was being obnoxious. If I heard 'That's because you're a Scorpio' one more time, I was going to get expelled."

"So what changed?"

My cheeks grow warm and I look away. "It turns out I was trying to make a long-term relationship work with my least compatible sign. That wasn't enough to make me a believer, but I like to be informed, so I did a few sessions with a relationship astrologist to learn about what I should be looking for going forward."

He seems to digest that information, then nudges my foot with his under the table. "Is Capricorn a good match?"

A slow smile spreads over my face. "Pretty good. *If* there's open communication."

"You mean like this?" He leans his elbows on the table, pinning me with a direct look. "I adore the taste of your cunt when you come on my face."

The air backs up in my lungs. I stare for a long moment, then burst out laughing. It's that or leap across the table and tear his pants off. "Duly noted."

He shrugs and chews another bite of steak. "Just communicating."

My pulse throbs as I watch him eat. His words have done the job. I'm not hungry for food anymore.

Fuck it. I push back my chair. Round the table. Straddle his lap. And kiss him.

Our mouths are salty and I don't care, because his hands are roaming my body, cupping, caressing, stroking.

He breaks the kiss to murmur against my mouth, "They're in the bedroom."

"What are?" I'm too busy trying to suck on his bottom lip. He groans and grasps my waist, grinding me down on his erection through the layers of our clothes.

His answer comes out as a scratchy hiss. "The nipple clamps."

"Oh. Right." Shit, I'd completely forgotten. Lightheaded, I climb off his lap and pull him to his feet. He leads me to his bedroom, which is stylishly decorated in slate blue and dove gray, before showing me the array of clamps spread out on his dresser.

I gulp, both at the thought of wearing them, and from the anticipation of seeing them on Gideon.

"Well." I pick up a clamp that looks like a silicone-tipped tweezer. "Shall we put those best practices to use?"

With a wolfish smile, he pulls me into another kiss.

It turns out I am not the biggest fan of nipple clamps. Gideon's gentle, and we keep up open communication, but I much prefer his mouth on my tits.

That said, the sight of Gideon with nipple adornments is a turn-on, especially since he picks ones that have a thin chain connecting them.

We try to time our orgasms with the moment we're supposed to remove the clamps, but it doesn't work, and having a phone timer ticking away the seconds stresses us out. By the time we're done, we both admit our nipples are sore.

"Two stars for wearing the clamps," Gideon says, lying flat on his back. Then he glances over at my reddened areolas, now decorated with his spend. "Five stars for the visual, though."

"Ditto. That little chain looked incredible on you." I lean over him and soothe his tender nips with my tongue. "Have you ever thought of piercing them?"

"No. Have *you?*"

"Once or twice."

He gets a speculative gleam in his eye, clearly imagining it.

And because it's on my mind, I add, "I forgot you pierced your ears senior year."

He seems surprised by the comment, and then his expression turns rueful as he runs his fingers through my hair. "A short-lived act of teenage rebellion. And maybe a desperate need to hint at my burgeoning queerness."

I raise my head from his chest to better look him in the eye. "How did that go over?"

He lets out a tired sigh. "Oh, the usual. My father threatened to disinherit me."

"For piercing your ears?" I stroke Gideon's lobes, noting the slight indentation in the center.

The look on his face is grim. "For daring to veer even slightly from the straight-and-narrow path of heteronormative masculinity he'd set forth for me."

My insides twist with compassion. I wish I could go back and hug the version of Gideon who'd wanted to express himself and been punished for it. I wish I could go back even further and be his friend. Sure, he'd been annoying, but I'd either ignored him or snapped back, unleashing my own inner bitch. It had never occurred to me that there might be more to him than met the eye.

But I can't go back. All we have is this moment, and what we choose to do with it.

So I kiss him. No tongue, no seduction, just a press of lips that I hope conveys some of what I'm feeling.

Not all of it. Shit, *I* don't even fully understand all of it. But I appreciate what he told me. And I appreciate that we're on this journey together.

I ease back before the kiss can deepen. His eyes are soft, his mouth pink.

Instead of kissing him again like I want to, I say, "Are you ready for the thing you've waited years to do?"

He gives me a heated look. "I've already fucked you, Valencia."

The words and the implication behind them, that he's wanted me for *years*, makes my toes curl, but I shake my head. "Not that. It's time for you to finally decorate your own Christmas tree, exactly the way you want."

"I think I'd rather fuck you again," he mutters, but he shifts to get off the bed. From there, we move companionably around his room and the adjoining bathroom while we clean up and get dressed.

It worries me that this man reentered my life just three days ago and I already feel so comfortable around him, but I put it out of my mind as I help him decorate.

The tree he bought is eight or nine feet tall, and I praise his skill in standing it up in the tree holder. He throws a cold french fry at me, and that sets the tone for the rest of the day. We joke about his "sturdy tree trunk" and hold ornaments in front of our nipples, as if we're considering piercing them. At some point over the past two days, Gideon picked up boxes of ornaments and decor from his mom's apartment, and as he opens them, I find years' worth of Andrea Noble's design trends.

"This is from the year everything was blood red," Gideon says, pulling out yards of thick ribbon. "And this was the year everything had gold stars."

"I do love getting a gold star," I tease, and he snickers.

By the time we're done and Gideon is stacking the bins of unused decorations, it's full dark out.

"I should get home," I say.

"Do you want to stay for dinner?"

I shake my head. "I have an early meeting in the morning, and my feet are pretty sore."

He walks me to the door, then holds my coat to help me into it. I slip my feet into my boots, which feel tighter than usual, thanks to the ice skates. I hold on to Gideon's arm while I zip them up.

"Soak them tonight," he murmurs. "With Epsom salts."

And even though there's nothing sexy about what he just said, a curl of desire unwinds in my belly. With both feet on the floor, I use his arm for leverage and press a quick kiss to his cheek. "Have a good day at work. I'll see you tomorrow night."

Then I yank open the door and hurry to the elevator before I can give in to the temptation to suggest we get a head start on tomorrow's activity.

Because tomorrow? Tomorrow we're playing with vibrators.

Chapter 10

GIDEON

Day 4: Vibrators & Hot Chocolate

It's cold on Monday night, but I bundle up after work and meet Valencia at the Union Square Holiday Market to wait on a long line for hot chocolate. Why? Because that's what she wants to do, and at this point, I'd swim naked in the East River if she put it on our list.

Yes, the *East* River, because I'm so fucking gone for this woman that I'd risk a bacterial infection to make her happy.

Luckily, all she wants tonight is overhyped cocoa, so here we are, winding our way through a warren of wooden stalls crammed into the southern end of Union Square Park, an area usually reserved for incense vendors, chess players, and protests. There are multiple booths that sell hot chocolate, but Valencia has done her research to find the *best* one.

"Not the one that's gone viral," she says as we join the line behind a trio of teenage girls. "There are a lot that rely on gimmicks, like sprinkles, or a marshmallow on a stick. But if we want just a good-quality cup of hot chocolate, apparently this is the place."

I adjust my scarf and nod. "I guess we'll be the judges of that."

The market is outdoors, but the stalls block the wind, and it's at least a couple of degrees warmer thanks to all the people packed into such tight quarters. I ask Valencia about her day and she's describing some of the bureaucratic challenges her department is facing when she suddenly stops. A slow smile spreads across her face as she peers behind me.

She grabs my arm before I can fully turn. "Shh. Listen."

I eavesdrop on the girls ahead of us, who are engaging in a serious debate about all the hot chocolate vendors present this year. As they launch into rating each on a scale of one to ten, I lock eyes with Valencia, who's shaking with suppressed laughter, and give her a stern look.

"We are not taste-testing every hot chocolate stand in this market."

She taps her chin with one gloved finger. "Now that you mention it . . ."

"No. It's not on the list." I lean down to murmur in her ear. "Besides, I have other items for you to test-drive tonight."

She gives me a sultry smile. "Items, plural?" When I nod, she adds, "You know I already have a couple of those *items*, right?"

The thought of her using a vibrator on herself makes me glad my coat comes down to midthigh. "You can never have too many. Or so I'm told."

She arches an eyebrow at me. "And who told you that?"

"My work husband."

"Oh, my God." She squeezes her eyes shut. "Did Rodrigo help you pick out these particular items?"

"What do you think?"

She tries to glare at me, but she's grinning.

By the time we get our hot chocolate, the temperature has dropped even further. We make our way to the statue of Gandhi, where there's a small space devoid of people. Just before we reach it, someone bumps into Valencia from behind. She drops her cup, letting out a dismayed cry as the nine-dollar hot chocolate we waited half an hour for splatters all over her boots.

I nearly crush my own cup as I spin toward the culprit, but they've already disappeared into the crowd. And besides, I won't leave Valencia, who's standing there with a disappointed pout, gazing down at the foamy brown liquid covering her feet and steaming on the ground.

"Come here." I slide an arm around her and lead her to the railing surrounding the statue. We reach it without further incident, but I keep her tucked against me. For warmth, for protection, hell, just for the feel of her. "Are you okay?"

"Yeah, just annoyed. These gloves are too thick, so I didn't have a good grip on it."

"Take them off," I say, passing her my cup. "We'll share mine."

It's a testament to how upset she is that she doesn't argue. She pulls off her gloves and lifts my cup to her mouth with both hands. After a long sip, her eyes flutter shut and her lips stretch in a satisfied smile.

"Ten out of ten," she whispers.

My heart lurches in my chest, and all I can do is whisper, "Yeah."

But I'm not talking about the cocoa.

When she hands the cup back to me, I take a small sip, but I'm so intent on watching her I could be drinking from a slush puddle and I wouldn't notice.

By the time Valencia drinks the last drop, I have her wrapped in a bear hug to keep her warm. She suggests we walk to her apartment, but the wind has picked up and she's shivering, so I hail a cab. I also suspect her feet are still sore from yesterday.

Once we're in her bedroom, I unpack half a dozen vibrating devices from an antimicrobial bag.

"They're clean and charged," I tell her. "Ready to go."

Valencia gapes at the array of sex toys on her dresser. "Um, wow."

One is a classic wand, with a bulbous head and a strong motor. Another has a fluttering tongue attachment. The next is shaped like a rosebud and was advertised as a "suction" vibe. I tried it on my palm and wasn't sure I understood it, but the sales clerk assured me it was a bestseller. Then there's a bullet with a soft silicone casing, and another you can wear on your finger that thumps against the clit.

And there's the ring, but that one's for me.

I cup her face with both hands and wait until she's looking at me. "Communication. You have to tell me what you like and don't like. Got it?"

She bites her lower lip and nods.

I hold up the first toy and the lube. "Ready?"

Her eyes meet mine, heavy-lidded but clear. "Yes."

The first we try is the fluttering one, but she says it's got nothing on my tongue. Two stars. We switch it out for the wand, which makes her come and gets four stars. The rose is a big hit and brings her to orgasm almost instantly. She gives it four and a half stars, then demands a break. I'm still fully dressed, but she's naked, so she throws on an oversize "Pan Pride" T-shirt and we eat leftover Chinese food while standing in her kitchen. She makes me tell her about my shopping trip with Rodrigo, and she's laughing on the way back to her bedroom. There, she marches over to the dresser and holds up the vibrating cock ring.

"Put it on," she demands. "Or do you think I didn't notice these are all for clitoral stimulation and the only way I'm getting stuffed tonight is with your dick?"

"Shit, don't say things like that if you still want me to be able to put it on." I hurry to lower my pants and maneuver my semihard erection through the ring. Once it's secured, I stroke myself to full hardness, groaning at the heightened pressure.

I hear a soft moan and look over to see a naked Valencia kneading her own breasts while she watches me. I quickly pull off my clothes and lie on my back, beckoning her to climb on. She moves eagerly, straddling my hips before wrapping her fingers around my cock. I let out a surprised grunt.

"Fuck, you're hard." She sounds breathy. "How do we turn this thing on?"

It takes both of us to figure it out, and we get sidetracked when Valencia takes me into her mouth, but once the ring is vibrating, she gets an excited gleam in her eye.

"This is going to be fun."

She holds me still, sinking down, and we groan in unison as I fill her.

She's so wet. So soft. So warm. I could stay here forever, buried in her cunt.

But that's not on the agenda. Valencia's inner walls clench around me and from there, it's a full-on fuckfest. We're both mindless with pleasure, slick with sweat. My hands grip her round ass cheeks, using them as leverage to rock her back and forth. Her clit grinds against the vibrating ring, and my dick strokes her inside. Our communication has devolved to groping and grunting, with the occasional "yes" and "please" and "fuck" and *"there."* Control shifts between us. Valencia takes over by rising to her knees and gyrating over the tip of my dick. Then it's my turn, and I brace my feet on the bed, thrusting into her from below.

And, bless her commitment to rule following, because she tells me *exactly* how good it feels, which is why I'm prepared when she squeezes around me like a vise. I grit my teeth, holding back my own orgasm as she digs her nails into my chest and emits a loud cry.

I have never seen anything more beautiful than Valencia Torres shattering on top of my cock, but that's not what sends me over the edge. No, what finally does it is her lips parting to reveal her tongue as it moves around the syllables of a single, silent word.

Gideon.

I yank her down to my chest, my arms locking around her as I lose it. Pleasure races in a current through my body, and I come with a shout. I might even lose consciousness for a second. But when I blink, I'm still lying down, and Valencia is still on top of me, breathing hard.

"Five stars for the vibrating cock ring," she says hoarsely against my collarbones. "Ten out of ten, would recommend."

"Couldn't agree more." My heart is trying to escape from my chest. "Fuck, you came so hard at the end, you almost pushed me out."

"My downstairs neighbor is probably going to complain about the screaming."

"Maybe if we give her the unused vibrators, she'll thank us instead."

"Gideon!" Valencia sputters out a laugh, and the corresponding spasm of her channel finally does push me out. We're both wet and sticky, but I don't care. I'm too busy trying to memorize the sound of my name on her tongue, the delighted smile spreading her lips.

I'm in so deep I can't see the surface, and I don't fucking care.

We clean up and I get dressed. She throws the T-shirt back on and walks me to the door. Before I leave, she pulls me in for a tight, friendly hug. I soak it in, then force myself to let go before I want to.

"Tomorrow night at my place, right?" I try to keep my tone light, but I also know it'll break me if she says no.

"I'll bring the wrapping paper." She opens the door. "Night, Gideon."

"Good night, Valencia." And then I call out, "Bye, Archie!"

She's laughing as she closes the door. Outside, I begin the walk home, grateful for the crisp night air. I need to clear my head.

Pulling out my phone, I text Rodrigo. You were right about the ring.

A reply from "Work Husband" pops up a second later. I fucking told you so!

Chapter 11

GIDEON

Day 5: Porn & Presents

Valencia, as it turns out, has a subscription to a female-focused ethical porn streaming service. She seems embarrassed as she rambles out an explanation.

"Earlier this year, after . . . Well, you know what happened. Anyway, this summer, I was embarking on my Hookup Era, and I'd never been with a woman before. But I wanted to, so . . ." She gestures at the girl-on-girl scene playing on my TV. "Research."

I want to ask about this Hookup Era, but all I say is, "I fucking love this about you."

Her cheeks go pink. "You just like the idea of me eating pussy."

My grin is wolfish. "That too."

While the women moan on-screen, Valencia and I gather everything in the living room. Since we're wrapping gifts for my firm's toy drive, I bought the presents, and Valencia brought wrapping supplies made from recycled materials.

As we sit on the floor to work, Valencia eyes the pile of Nintendo Switches, iPads, and LEGO sets. "Don't you think you went overboard with the gifts?"

"Valencia, look who you're talking to."

She snorts. "Remind me again why you work?"

"Because I don't like being bored." I glance at the TV and cringe. "How is that comfortable?"

Valencia tilts her head, mimicking the awkward angle of the upside-down woman's neck. "She must do yoga."

We get started, and to my surprise, Valencia is . . . not the best at wrapping gifts. I, having been trained by Andrea Noble herself, wrap with the precision of an origami master. Or close to it. It's nice to know Valencia isn't perfect at something. Not so I can make fun of her, like I would have once upon a time, but just to know that she's human.

I want to ask if she needs help, but I bite my tongue. Instead, I listen to her muttered curses, which sometimes mirror those of the women on-screen. Finally, Valencia tosses down a roll of eco-friendly ribbon and glares at me.

"Show me how to do it," she demands, and I hide a smile.

I show her the way my mom taught me—measuring the right amount of paper, then folding the edges and creasing them with a fingernail before applying tape. Once she's got it, she takes over wrapping while I handle ribbons and bows.

A threesome scene comes on next, and I watch idly out of the corner of my eye.

"Why no swords crossing?" I ask.

Valencia shrugs. "Missed opportunity."

I turn the volume down. The woman in this scene is pretty loud, but I guess I would be too if I had two dicks in me.

Valencia passes me a wrapped iPad. "My mom always did this part," she says quietly.

"Wrapping gifts?" I want to make sure I'm following.

She nods. "Mom was so creative. I wish I'd inherited that from her."

"First of all, our list is *extremely* creative. And second, I'd wager you got more from her than you realize."

She shoots me a grateful look. "I just thought I had more time, you know? It was so sudden."

"Did you talk to anyone about it? After?"

"I did grief counseling for a while. It helped. Maybe I should revisit it. The shock, and then being the only one left to manage everything . . . That was really hard. Like I said, I probably leaned on the Mulhollands too much. But they helped me with the paperwork and were really supportive. I'm not sure how I would've gotten through it without them."

I wonder how much of her attachment to Mulholland was about his parents, but I don't ask. The fact that she seems to be more upset about missing Christmas with them than lamenting the dissolution of her engagement is pretty telling.

"But I guess losing a parent is never easy. With your father, was it . . ." She trails off, like she's afraid to ask for details. And while it's painful, I don't mind telling her. After all, she knows this particular grief well.

"It was a pretty rapid decline. Only three months from the time he found out he was sick. And he didn't tell me, initially. He'd known for a month before I figured it out and asked my mom. So for me, it was more like two months."

It hadn't been enough time for me to wrap my head around it, to come to grips with watching him waste away, then scrambling to pack in a lifetime's worth of closure with a man who had no real interest in it.

"He did say he was proud of me," I say quietly. "During our last two-sided conversation, before he couldn't talk anymore. He said he was proud of me, but I don't . . . I don't know if he meant it. Sometimes I think he just said it because he was dying."

She doesn't speak for a while, just keeps wrapping, before she asks, "Does it matter?"

I shake my head ruefully. "My therapist has asked me that so many fucking times."

"And?"

I heave a sigh, and my gaze flicks to the TV, where the woman is getting spit roasted. Shaking my head, I look away. "No, it doesn't matter. Even if he only said it because he was dying, he still thought to say it. And it doesn't matter that he did, because I can't live my life to try to make him proud. It was impossible then, and it's even more impossible now. I can only try to be proud of myself."

Her eyes shine as she presses her lips together. Finally, she whispers, "I really want to say I'm proud of you, but that seems counterproductive."

I open my mouth to tell her that maybe it shouldn't mean anything to me, but it *does*. But at that very moment, the woman on screen yells, "Do it! Fuck my little holes with those monster cocks!"

There's a beat of silence. Valencia and I stare at the TV, then we both burst out laughing.

"This is too weird!" Valencia digs through a pile of discarded wrapping paper for the remote. "I can't talk about grief and wrap a walking, talking Elmo during a DP scene. I'm sorry, I just can't do it."

I shudder as she hits pause. "I thought this would be sexy, but it just feels *wrong*."

"I'm putting on a movie instead." She navigates to the dashboard and picks *The Muppet Christmas Carol*.

"Excellent choice, but this doesn't count toward Day 10." I jab a finger at her. "You're not getting out of our agreement early."

"Don't worry," she says breezily. "We're still on for movies this weekend."

We wrap presents while Valencia sings along with the movie. She knows every word, and it's fucking adorable. Her voice isn't very strong, but she can carry a tune, and there's something pleasant about tying elaborate bows and thinking about the child who'll open this gift, while Valencia sings "One More Sleep 'til Christmas" with Kermit the Frog.

When the song ends, she passes me another box. "Does your firm do this toy drive every year?"

"Yeah. Rodrigo's in charge of it."

She side-eyes me. "You give money, too, don't you?"

"I can confirm that a monetary donation is also made on behalf of the Noble Foundation."

"The Noble Foundation." She repeats it under her breath, but she's smiling. I have a feeling she's going to look it up, so I save her the trouble.

"Do you want to see the press release listing our other charitable donations from the year?"

"Actually, I would." She gives me a sunny smile. "And then I have a list of environmental groups you should recommend for next year."

"Consider it done."

She stares at me. "Just like that?"

"Just like that." It's funny that she thinks there's anything I wouldn't do for her. "My mother and I are the ones who make those decisions now. And she doesn't require convincing the way my . . ."

I can't finish the sentence, but I don't have to. Valencia pats my knee, and when a new song begins, she sings along with gusto. In between songs, we talk about work. She tells me about the Clean Air Act presentation she's giving tomorrow, and I talk about a win with my latest immigration case.

Once all the presents are wrapped, she holds up three fingers. "Wrapping presents—three stars."

I frown. "Only three?"

"I don't like things I'm bad at."

"What about wrapping presents while watching porn?"

"Ugh, zero stars." She makes a face, then purses her lips in thought. "I'd watch porn with you under different circumstances, but we should've paired it with another prompt, like baking."

"Maybe we can try a do-over," I say, testing the waters, but all she says is, "Maybe! What about you?"

"Me?"

"How would you rate the evening?"

I pause, then blurt out, "Five stars. For wrapping presents while you sing along with the Muppets."

She smiles. "You charmer."

As I walk her to the door, I realize that we didn't even have sex tonight. And despite how absolutely ravenous I am for her, I don't feel like there was anything missing. It was enough to spend time with her, even if things were sort of awkward, what with the porn and the presents and the discussion of dead parents. But *we* weren't awkward. We got through all of it, together, and I'll see her tomorrow. And the next day, and the next, and every day until Christmas Eve.

Still, I pull her in for a goodbye kiss before she leaves. I don't mean to make it sexy, but once we start, I can't let go. I slant my mouth over hers, changing the angle, and she opens for me. Before I know it, she's nipping at me with her teeth, and I'm sliding my knee between her thighs.

"Oh, fuck, Gideon," she rasps, grinding her pussy against my leg. "Damn, that's good."

I growl in response, since my mouth is busy trailing sucking kisses down her throat. I'm hard for the first time all night as I tug her scarf aside and scrape my teeth over her clavicle. I *adore* the sounds she makes when I do this.

I'm reaching for the zipper on her coat when I stop myself.

"Go." I grip her arms and maneuver her away from me. "Go, before I . . ." Fuck, I don't even know what. Before I beg her to stay? "Text me when you get home."

Her lips are swollen, her eyes glassy. "Yeah. Okay."

"I hope your presentation goes well tomorrow."

"Yeah. Tomorrow." She nods, still looking dazed. "Thanks."

I want to walk her home, but if I do, we'll end up in her bed. So I just open the door and give her a smirk full of all the pent-up desire raging through my system. "Good night, Valencia."

Her voice has a dreamy quality to it. "Good night, Gideon."

I close the door behind her and lock it, then drag my hands down my face.

I'm tempted to turn the porn back on and jerk off, but I don't. The anticipation won't kill me. And besides, I have a surprise planned for her.

Whistling the finale song from the movie, I head to my bedroom to set up.

Chapter 12

Valencia

Day 6: Role-Play & Window Displays

The department store windows along Fifth Avenue this year feature an odd and probably unintentional commentary on female archetypes—Greek goddesses, women in STEM careers, and Mrs. Claus's kitchen—but I like walking arm in arm with Gideon, and his sharp wit makes for excellent entertainment.

It's also a much-needed counterpoint to our conversation last night. I never would've thought my archnemesis would be so easy to open up to, and I find myself needing emotional distance. A crowded, outdoor activity and adventures in role-play are just the thing to get this Naughty and Nice List back on track.

When we get to Gideon's apartment, he surprises me with a pair of matching, sexy reindeer costumes. He's also decorated his bedroom to look like the North Pole, with fake snow, a six-foot-tall candy cane pointing the way to Santa's Workshop, and an inflatable snowman like you'd see on someone's front lawn.

It's excessive and kind of ridiculous, but also sweet and thoughtful, and that, as I'm discovering, is Gideon to a T.

"Someone's been a busy little elf." I shoot him a sassy smile over my shoulder as I stroll around his room. I'm wearing what looks like a velour one-piece swimsuit with ribbons that tie behind my neck. It's tan with white fur trim, white appliqué spots on the hips, and a surprisingly realistic-looking tail on the butt. Conveniently, the garment has three snaps at the crotch, like a baby onesie, for greater ease when peeing or fucking, I presume.

"I needed to set the stage for our reindeer games," he says, and I snort-laugh. "Do you like your costume?"

"I do. Although when I wrote this prompt down, I expected some kind of classroom fantasy. Plaid skirt, bending over a desk, that sort of thing."

His eyes glow with promise. "Next time."

He comes up behind me, and we grin at our reflections in the mirror. We look so fucking silly. His costume consists of tan shorts with white fur trim and a tail just like mine. On top, there's only a red harness with jingle bells dangling from it. We both wear headbands with felt antlers and ears attached.

I strike a pose. "*This* is what we should've worn to Dazzler."

"We would've fit right in. Especially with this."

He holds up a red foam Rudolph nose, which sparks a very lawyerly debate over who will wear it. I put forth the argument that as the bullied one in this scenario, I'll be more in tune with the character. Gideon asserts that Rudolph is unquestionably a top, and therefore, *he* should be the most famous reindeer of all. I really just want to see Gideon wear the nose, so I let him win.

"If you're Rudolph, then who am I?" I ask, pouting.

Gideon rakes me with a scorching look. "*Vixen*, obviously."

We do it "reindeer-style" in front of his bedroom mirror while the snowman looks on. Gideon's Rudolph nose falls off almost immediately and rolls under the bed. My antlers end up around my neck. The jingling of his harness marks the rhythm of his thrusts, and I don't think I'll ever hear sleigh bells again without remembering this moment.

We laugh the entire time, and whenever he calls me "Vixen" in a sultry growl, my knees go weak.

It is, by far, the most fun I've ever had during a sexual encounter.

But afterward, once I've changed back into my sweater and jeans and Gideon has gone into the kitchen to make us tea, I can't help but feel that while we might've gotten the list back on track, my emotions are still very much speeding in a direction I don't want them to go.

I'm sitting on his sofa, making room in my shoulder bag for the reindeer antlers, when Gideon sets two mugs on the glass coffee table.

"What's that?" He reaches into the bag and pulls out the book I'm reading, a psychological thriller that's currently topping the bestseller lists. "I've seen ads for this one. How is it?"

"The main character makes some stupid decisions, but it's definitely a page-turner."

"How so?"

"Well . . . here. Let me read you this part."

We sit side by side on the sofa while I flip back a few pages. I read him the scene where the protagonist finally accepts that someone has it out for her, and when I'm done, he asks me to keep going.

Soon, we're both absorbed in the story—I wasn't lying, it's compelling as hell—and Gideon's stretched out on the sofa with his head in my lap. We've finished our tea, and I'm playing with his hair, sliding my fingers through the cool strands as I read aloud in a low voice. It isn't until he emits a soft snore that I realize he's fallen asleep.

After all we've done together over the past six days—and I can't believe it's *only* been six days—this is the first time I've seen him sleeping.

His brow is smooth, not a trace of tension or the grief I sometimes see weighing on him. I recognize it, because it's something I carry with me, too. But now, his expression is peaceful, the lines of his face sharp and beautiful, his lower lip resplendent in repose. If I had the skill, I'd write sonnets to that mouth.

Or love songs.

My stomach drops like I'm on a roller coaster as emotions that have nothing to do with lists or sex or Christmas spiral through me.

Shit, I'm in so much trouble.

"Wake up, sleepyhead." I give in to the urge to stroke his cheek, feeling faint stubble.

He leans into the touch, making a purring sound reminiscent of Archie. It's too fucking endearing. I have to get out of here.

"It's getting late," I say, but he doesn't sit up. Instead, his arms wind around my waist and he nuzzles my stomach.

"But you're so comfortable." The words come out petulant and muffled, and his breath warms my skin through the weave of my sweater.

Fuck me. Why does he have to be so cute? I squeeze my eyes shut and search for my resolve. "I have work in the morning."

With a resigned sigh, he finally releases me. I slide the book into my bag and hurry to the door.

My boots are on and I'm zipping my coat when he comes up beside me.

"Coming over for your spanking tomorrow?" His tone is husky, and he smothers a yawn.

I respond with a cheeky grin. "No, I'm coming over to deliver *your* spanking, you naughty boy."

He winces, and I laugh. It feels like we're back on solid ground.

But then he cups my shoulders and lays the sweetest kiss on me, a gentle press of lips that says way more than I want it to, and I fucking melt.

Break the kiss! I scream at myself, but I can't.

Gideon steps back first, his teeth dragging over his lower lip as he gives me a sleepy smile.

And with that enticing image burned into my brain, I blurt out "Bye!" and rip open the door. I dash into the hallway and pound the elevator button, needing to escape before I do something stupid, like stay and never leave.

That was my problem with Everett. I didn't know when to leave.

Stick to sex, I tell myself. *That's all you have time for anyway.*

Still, it isn't our "reindeer games" replaying in my mind as I walk home, but Gideon snuggling against me as he slept.

Chapter 13

Gideon

Day 7: Spanking & Spiked Cider

"What do you mean she *read* to you? Is this some kind of library kink?"

I shoot Rodrigo an irritated look as we leave the office and hurry to the subway. I've been trying to explain last night without admitting how fucking *nice* it was to fall asleep on Valencia, but Rodrigo keeps interrupting. "No, she read a *book* to me, and—never mind. Why do I tell you anything?"

"Because I'm your work husband." Rodrigo blows me a kiss, but then his expression turns serious. "Look, all kidding aside, this seems really fast. You've been spending every second with this woman, after not seeing her for nearly a decade, and the only thing you'll say about that time is that you 'weren't really friends.'" Even his air quotes look sarcastic. "Forgive me for worrying about your depressed ass."

Rodrigo is too emotionally intelligent. It makes him a great friend—excuse me, a great *work husband*—but it means I can't hide shit from him. After my father died, I'd probably have turned into a recluse who never left the apartment if it hadn't been for Rodrigo.

But he's right. Valencia and I are halfway through our list, and I can barely remember what my life was like before she came back into it. All I did was work, exercise, occasionally grab drinks with my colleagues—oh, and have weekly sessions with Ralph. Can't forget those.

"Bailey moved in with you after a week," I retort, because defensiveness is all I have at this point.

"That was different."

"How?"

"It wasn't *official*. He just never left. And don't change the subject. Has Valencia shown signs that she wants to extend your kinky advent calendar past Christmas?"

I grit my teeth. "No."

"Have you dropped hints?"

I sigh. "Yes."

"Listen, I just don't want you to get—"

"*Bye*, Rodrigo," I say pointedly, breaking off and jogging down the subway steps at Wall Street.

"Just ask her!" he yells, but I'm already underground.

I'm too nervous to do tonight's activity under the influence, so Valencia is meeting me at my apartment before we go out for drinks. She arrives ten minutes after I do, and we get started right away.

I've done research, so I know to get Valencia revved up beforehand. But to my surprise, when I show her the mini riding crop I bought, she insists I use my hand instead—on her ass *and* her tits. I can't lie, it's kind of hot, but I'm afraid of hurting her, even though she assures me that I can smack her ass a little harder while I fuck her.

She, however, has no qualms about using the crop on me and turning my butt as red as Santa's suit. But considering she's also working my lubed cock with quick strokes of her fist, I barely notice.

Later, however, when we finally get into Rolf's German Restaurant and take our seats on the high wooden bar stools, I'm definitely aware of the sting. Good thing tomorrow's activity isn't butt plugs. My ass needs a break.

Rolf's is known for its bountiful Christmas decor and holiday cocktails. Valencia orders the hot spiked cider, and I go for the vanilla-spiced eggnog with bourbon. While she visits the restroom, I text a picture of the ceiling to Rodrigo. It's heavy with lights, baubles, plastic icicles, and vintage ornaments. Porcelain dolls hover among the pine boughs like the restless ghosts of Victorian children. I can't deny that it's atmospheric, somehow managing to be both cozy and overwhelming at the same time.

I hear Valencia's voice a few minutes later. Out of the corner of my eye, I recognize who she's talking to, and my blood runs cold.

It's Fern Mulholland.

Fern's hair is platinum now instead of brown, but her sprite-like face and smoky voice are unmistakable. She's farther down the bar with her arm around another woman. I strain my ears and catch Fern introducing her date to Valencia. Then Fern lets out a little laugh and says, "For a second I thought you were sitting with Gideon Noble."

My body goes numb. There's a long pause, and I fully expect Valencia to deny it. She has the perfect opportunity to say, "Of course not, don't be silly," and go, leaving me behind.

But Valencia, as always, is stronger than I give her credit for. "I am."

Fern's smile drops off her face comically fast. She blinks a few times, then whispers, *"Valencia."*

There's a wealth of feeling in the way she says the name, and it cuts me to the core. It would be easier if Fern launched into a litany of recriminations. But this one word, uttered with a combination of disbelief and censure and dismay, is a thousand times worse.

Because she doesn't actually *need* to say anything. Valencia already knows. Hell, *I* know.

But Valencia still doesn't deny it. Doesn't deny *me*.

It warms the cold place deep inside me, moves me more than it should. If I had any decency, I'd get up now and leave. Not just the restaurant, but leave Valencia alone for good, like I tried to do in high school. She doesn't need me and all my baggage weighing her down.

I sneak another glance while pretending to text, but all I can see is Fern's concerned expression and the back of Valencia's hair.

"Are you sure you know what you're—"

"I'm *fine*." Valencia says it firmly, and I would sell my soul to see her face right now. "You don't need to worry about me."

Fern's features soften and she places a hand on Valencia's arm. "I know. But I do anyway."

Valencia's posture eases almost imperceptibly. "You're a good friend, Fern Mulholland."

At that, Fern winces. "I'll leave it to you to tell Ev about this."

A chill goes down my back, and I'm relieved when Valencia shakes her head.

"I have nothing to say to him. Besides, it's none of his business who I spend my time with."

My chest swells with pride. Pride in Valencia for standing up for herself. And also, maybe, a bit for myself. To know that someone like Valencia Torres accepts me . . . I don't even have the words for what it means to me.

So I'll just have to show her. Somehow.

But then Valencia says something that gives me what can only be described as a hot flash. "Why don't you come over and say hi to him?"

My muscles tense as the two women approach. I greet Fern with a wary nod. "FernGully."

She responds with an impish grin. "Hey, Knobble."

I groan at the mocking childhood nickname, even though I had it coming. "God, I haven't heard that one in years."

"Always happy to remind you of what a scumbag you were," she says cheerfully. "You take care of my girl here, all right?" Fern points two fingers at her eyes and then at me in an I'm-watching-you gesture. Then she gives Valencia a peck on the cheek and returns to her date.

I sag against the bar. "Well, that didn't go as disastrously as it could have."

Valencia takes her seat next to me. "I thought for sure she'd call you something worse."

I nod, but seeing Fern is a reminder of our pasts, and glaring proof that we don't exist in an eggnog-and-sex-soaked bubble.

Rodrigo's parting words from earlier come back to me. *Just ask her.*

Rejection isn't a death sentence, right? At least, that's what Ralph always says. I take a deep breath and blurt out, "What are we doing here, Valencia?"

She glances up, her brow creased in confusion. "Having thirty-dollar drinks."

"No, I mean, us. What are *we* doing? Together."

Her expression turns guarded. "We're working our way through our list."

"And?" I need to know if she's as invested as I am.

She toys with the thin gold bracelet circling her wrist. "I can only answer for myself. I'm here because I don't want to be alone at Christmastime. I'm here because, despite everything, you're funny and hot and great in bed, and we have a good time together. I'm here because we made a plan and it has been the bright spot in an otherwise dismal year, and I'm committed to seeing it through. Beyond that?" She gives a tired shrug, and finally looks at me. "I don't know, Gideon. That has to be enough for now."

Her words are like an icicle in my chest, cold and sharp and deadly, but I only nod. Sure, her response was layered in compliments, but the bottom line was clear: Christmas Eve is our termination date.

I open my mouth—to say what, I have no idea—but she pins me with a steely look. "I have a question for you, too."

I can already tell I'm not going to like it, but she answered me honestly, and I can only do the same. "Shoot."

"What does your therapist think about us?"

I cough. "While I suspect Ralph doesn't think it's the smartest choice, he hasn't come right out and said so."

She taps her lip in thought. "I figured he wouldn't agree with you making a sex pact with someone you used to hate."

I frown. "I didn't hate you."

"No?" From her tone, I can tell this has been bothering her. I meet her gaze and try to let her see everything I'm feeling so there's no misunderstanding.

"Never. Not even when you had the nerve to get prettier and more brilliant every year."

Her lips press together like she's fighting a grin. "Fine. But what about now? What did you think when you saw me at the bar?"

"Fishing for compliments?"

"Only if you mean them."

I lean closer, lowering my voice and sliding one hand up the back of her cherry red sweater to cup her nape. "I thought you had the sexiest fucking neck I'd ever seen, and that I couldn't remember the last time I'd felt so attracted to anyone. And even if you laughed in my face, I needed to talk to you." I release her and sit back, but leave my hand at her waist. "And then you turned around."

She laughs. "That must have been horrifying."

Before I can say that it was probably the best moment of my life, the bartender plops our drinks down, and I don't get the chance. Valencia insists we take a ton of photos, and when she's satisfied with the results, we finally tap our glasses together and drink.

My eggnog is served in a wineglass with ice cubes and has a cinnamon stick floating on top. It's creamy and strong and packed with holiday spices. We swap and I taste Valencia's spiked cider—warm and tart—before I return to the topic at hand.

"All right, same question. What did you think when you saw me?" I've been wanting to know since the first night, and if all I have left with her are a handful of days, I might as well ask.

Her gaze flits over my face, soft as a caress. "That you'd grown up handsome. And there was . . . I dunno, a vulnerability in you that hadn't been there before."

She always did see too much. Or maybe I'm not as good at hiding things as I thought.

"You used to hate me, too." I don't like saying it, but I feel compelled to get everything out in the open.

She shakes her head. "I actually didn't. I resented how you treated me, but . . . it was closer to pity than contempt."

I groan. "I think that's worse."

"Is it?" Her compassionate tone makes me stop and consider.

Maybe it isn't worse. Maybe it meant she saw underneath the sneering facade to someone who was insecure and scared and unhappy. Someone whose parents hadn't done right by him, as Ralph often points out.

"I don't deserve you," I whisper, and her mouth twists.

"Gideon, I need to know . . . Are you sure being with me isn't some path to redemption or a manifestation of self-loathing?"

My stomach feels hollow. God, if that's what she thinks, no wonder she doesn't see a future for us. "No. Is that what it is for you?"

"I don't hate myself, Gideon." She says it gently, and the implication is that I do.

And honestly, I do hate myself for everything I said and did in an effort to be the son my father wanted me to be. What better way to spite my dead dad than to take up with the extraordinary girl who'd drawn his ire, the target of my own childish taunts? What better method of self-flagellation?

Except while I might hate what I did and who I'd been, I'm not here now out of some misguided attempt to get back at my father, and I'm not trying to fuck my way to forgiveness.

"So why *are* you here?" she asks softly, and I give the question due consideration.

The simplest answer is that I want to be.

Why? Because I *like* her. Beyond the physical attraction. Beyond the combustible chemistry. I like her wit and her sharp mind. I like her prim tone and her lusty sighs. I like that she doesn't shy away from what needs to be said or done, and I like that she's practical and hardworking but also playful and fun.

The patient understanding in her eyes nearly masks the uncertainty lurking there. She's so strong, but with a soft, caring, and compassionate heart beating beneath the armor. Once I would have sneered at it as a weakness, but now I know it's her greatest strength.

I drag in a breath. Being vulnerable does *not* come easily to me, is in fact something I've avoided for nearly my whole life.

But I'm trying to change, right? To grow. To be better.

Even if this isn't going anywhere, I promised to communicate. So I do.

"It's you. I just like being with you."

To my surprise, she scoffs. "No, you don't. I'm a bossy smart-ass, remember? That hasn't changed."

"But I have," I say seriously. "And the bossy smart-ass thing is a turn-on."

She still looks skeptical, so I take her hand.

"What you said earlier, about not wanting to be alone for the holidays? It's enough." I hold her gaze as I press a slow kiss to her knuckles. "For now."

It isn't, but if she doesn't want to pursue this any further, I have to be okay with it.

Even if it destroys me, as Ralph seems worried it will.

The bartender asks pointedly if we want anything else, so we take that as our cue to leave. Outside, a light snow has started to fall, and I order a car for Valencia. If left to her own devices, she'll walk, and if I bring her home, I'll try to stay.

After the conversation we just had, I think we both need space.

I'm warming her hands between my own when her car arrives, and then I lean down to kiss her forehead. "Until tomorrow."

She nods and squeezes my hand. "I'll meet you at Rockefeller Center."

As I'm getting into my own taxi, I realize we haven't rated any of our activities in days.

I don't let myself read anything into it. Instead, I text Rodrigo.

She said no.

Chapter 14

Day 8: Blindfolds & the Rockettes

It's Friday, my last day of work for the year, and I spend it dissecting my conversation with Gideon.

The small part of me that worried this was just a prolonged hate-fuck has been laid to rest. But when he asked what we were doing, all I could hear was Everett's voice, saying shit like, "Why be in a relationship if you're not going to make time for it?"

Sure, things are great with Gideon *now*, but what happens in the new year when I'm neck-deep in projects again? Because it doesn't matter how much I enjoy being with him, or that my heart skipped a beat when he said he liked me. Making a joke was easier than facing his earnest declaration or trying to continue this and realizing we can't make it work.

But we have tickets tonight for the Radio City Christmas Spectacular, one of Gideon's only holiday suggestions for our list. Even with my thoughts in turmoil, I'm looking forward to it.

For the occasion, I buy a long-sleeved wrap dress in emerald green velvet, a nod to the one I wore in eighth grade. I cover it up with my black wool coat and take the subway to meet Gideon at an Italian restaurant in Rockefeller Center.

When he sees me in the dress, his jaw goes slack. "God, look at you. Did you wear this for me?"

The rasp in his voice and his stunned expression make my pulse race.

"Maybe," I say primly, taking the seat he's pulled out. The hungry look he sends me has nothing to do with the scents of garlic and basil in the air.

Still, the meal is delicious, and after we leave, we stop to take selfies in front of Rockefeller Center's eighty-foot Christmas tree.

Gideon stands behind me, his arms wrapped around my middle and his cheek pressed to mine. Even though my arms are far shorter than his, I extend one and hold my phone out to take the photo. With my other hand, I cup the side of his face.

"Smile."

He does.

The photo is so perfect, it hurts.

"Send it to me," he says, and then he catches my hand in his and pulls me down the sidewalk toward Radio City Music Hall.

I've never seen the Rockettes perform live, and the show is aptly named because it is indeed a *spectacle*. There's dancing and singing, music and projections, and a whole lot of Santas. At one point, when I look over at Gideon, I could swear his eyes are glittering. But after it's over and I ask him what he thought, all he says is, "A little cornier than I remembered. But the production was incredible, and the synchronization is truly impressive."

I suspect the show affected him more than he's letting on, so as we wait for our ride, I aim for irreverence.

"You should join the Rockettes."

That jolts him out of his reverie. "I should what?"

"You heard me." I poke his thigh. "They're like a flock of beautiful flamingos, and you'd fit right in with these killer gams."

Just as I hoped, he bursts into laughter, so I keep it up. "What's it like having long legs? That's not a joy I'll ever experience."

He gazes down at me with a fond smile. "I like your legs exactly as they are."

I melt a little inside. "Right answer."

The car brings us back to my place, where I pour us glasses of red wine. We sit on my sofa with Archie purring between us. Gideon has loosened his tie, but there's tension in the lines of his face and the set of his broad shoulders.

I stretch my arm over the back of the couch and stroke the hair at the nape of his neck. He closes his eyes and leans into my touch.

"Was it difficult? Seeing the show?" A week ago I wouldn't have asked, but I haven't known him for a week, I've known him for sixteen years. And right now, I feel closer to him than anyone else in my life.

I don't question why that's true. It just is.

"It was more . . . complicated . . . than I was expecting." He opens his eyes, his gaze solemn. "I'm glad you were with me."

My mouth tightens into a little frown. "Maybe we should've done something else."

"No. It was a perfect night." Despite his words, frustration colors his tone. "I'm just . . . me, I guess. And no matter where I go, or what I'm doing, I can't leave all my bullshit behind."

My heart breaks, even as I leap to defend him. "It's not bullshit. You're allowed to have feelings, even complicated ones."

He looks so forlorn I'm about to suggest we skip tonight's other activity. But then he sets his wine down and with slow, deliberate movements, undoes the knot in his tie. His eyes never leave mine, and even though he hasn't said anything, my heart rate speeds up.

He slides the column of charcoal gray silk from around his neck and holds it taut between his big, strong hands.

"Day 8," he says in a deep voice. "Blindfold."

In the past, just the idea of being blindfolded would've made me anxious. But I feel safe with Gideon, and I suspect that tonight, he needs me to show that I trust him.

So I lift my chin ever so slightly, and he takes it for the invitation it is.

The loss of one sense heightens the others, and after he lays me on my bed, I lose track of how many orgasms he wrings from me with his mouth and hands. He's so careful, constantly checking in, and I've never felt more protected.

Finally, Gideon's hips settle between my legs and his heavy cock rests on my mound.

"Let me in?" He must be out of his mind with need, but he says it tenderly.

I find the strength to hitch my thighs over his hips, nudging his taut ass with my heels. I'm open and wet, more than ready for him. His arms wind around my back and he plunges into me. I cling to him like ivy on a brick wall, using my sense of touch to form a mental picture of him on top of me. *In* me.

And then I'm lost to everything except the pounding of his cock and the sweet words he whispers darkly in my ear.

"God, Valencia. Seeing you in that dress . . . I wanted to tear it off you, right in the fucking restaurant. You are everything I've ever wanted. You know that? I'll never get enough of you. Never, never, *never*."

He punctuates the statement with thrusts, and I nearly burst with the sense of my own power. *I* do this to him. *Me*, Valencia Torres. His ferocity unleashes an answering force in me, and I thrash my head, loving the delicious tug on my scalp from his fist wrapped around my hair.

Without warning, he pushes off me. I experience a moment of uncertainty, not sure where he's going, before he hitches up one of my knees. His hips pin me to the bed. The heel of his hand grinds circles against my clit as his strokes hit deep inside.

Oh, this is good. *Too* good. I'm unraveling in the dark, my hands scrabbling against his toned back.

"Come, my sweet little vixen," he croons. "You can do it. Come for me."

His hoarse whisper burrows into the place where all my unnamed feelings hide. For a second, I'm afraid they'll spill out.

I rip off the blindfold, needing his face to ground me. Blinking in the soft light, I soak in the way he grits his teeth, the way his brow creases like he's in pain, and then the way those luscious fucking lips form his next words.

"You have no goddamn clue what you do to me, Valencia."

I don't, but oh, I want to.

I can't ask, though, because the orgasm bears down on me. I cry out, clenching around him. His whole body stiffens. He gives a series of powerful thrusts, then releases a staccato groan that echoes the tremors in my core.

With a heavy exhale, he drops to the bed, then gathers me against his side.

We're panting and staring at each other, our faces just inches apart.

Something is different now. I don't know what, or why, and part of me doesn't want to know. Especially after I told him last night that we don't have a future past the end of our list.

But the other part, the part that *does* understand what's changed, speaks. "Stay here tonight."

His voice is quiet when he answers, his expression raw and unguarded. "I want to. More than anything."

I swallow hard. "But?"

"Today brought up a lot of memories. I need to run, and there's a good chance I'll toss and turn all night. I don't want to subject you to that."

My heart breaks for him. "I can handle it."

"You shouldn't have to." He gives me a small smile. "Besides, you're staying at my place tomorrow. I don't want you to get sick of me."

Never, I think, but I'm not ready to say it. Instead, I kiss the freckles on his nose. And when he pulls away to slide off the bed, I let him go.

Chapter 15

Gideon

Day 9: Butt Plugs & Baking

Valencia asked me to stay. And I said *no*.

That knowledge eats away at me all Saturday morning. I hate that I couldn't spend the night with the woman I . . . adore . . . because my demons caught up to me. After I left her, I ran on the treadmill until I'd exhausted myself and still slept poorly.

But Valencia is spending the whole weekend with me, and I'm determined not to let the past interfere.

In a move I now regret, I gave Rodrigo's number to Valencia, and the two of them went shopping for butt plugs together. The ones Valencia bought are red and green with heart-shaped plastic crystals on the bases. She presents them to me after a day of baking gingerbread and drinking coquito, a Puerto Rican holiday drink that's heavy on the rum.

"We're really doing this?" I sigh, like Rodrigo didn't book me a last-minute wax just for the occasion.

"Oh, yeah." Her dark eyes gleam with merriment. "We are really doing this."

I've been on the giving end of anal a few times—with men and women—but never the receiving end. We've both researched best practices, and the plugs Valencia bought are for beginners, but I'm still nervous.

Since I skipped the blindfold last night, I let her insert mine first. The plug is overwhelming, but in a good way, and it intensifies the pleasure when I fuck her from behind, especially with the enticing visual of that red heart-shaped gem in her cute little asshole.

But then Valencia says something that knocks me for a loop. "Gideon, I want to try."

My brain and hips stutter to a halt. "Try . . . ?"

She peers at me over her shoulder, her cheek pressed to the bed. "I don't know if I'll ever do this level of prep again, so we might as well do it."

I attempt to clarify. "By *it*, you mean . . ."

I can't get the words out, but she nods anyway. "Please."

Please. She wants me to *please* fuck her in the ass.

My whole body alights with fierce anticipation, but I manage to keep my voice steady. "All right."

I pull out of her, because I can't think straight while buried in her cunt. Carefully grasping the jeweled base of her plug, I tug on it gently, teasing her as it slides free. She gives a soft gasp, but I don't pause. I spit on her asshole and slip the tip of my wet thumb inside.

She whimpers, arching back against me, and I bite off a groan. She's so fucking tight, clamping around me as I push deeper.

"Oh, God. This might be too much."

"Easy, Vixen," I breathe, slowly sliding my thumb in and out. My other fingers grip the curve of her ass cheek for leverage. "How's it feel?"

"It's . . . it's good," she whispers.

"Ready for more?" When she nods, I add lube and replace my thumb with my index and middle fingers, stretching her.

She gives a sharp hiss and her shoulders hunch. "I'm okay," she says when I pause. "It's just . . . full."

The way she says *full* makes me shiver. "Keep communicating with me. And if you change your mind—"

"I know." She smiles at me over her shoulder. "I trust you."

That unleashes an avalanche of emotion in me, but despite our agreement, I can't confess what's on the tip of my tongue.

Instead, I tell her how beautiful she is and how well she's taking my fingers, how good I'm going to make her feel, and how hard I'm going to come in her ass. I say a lot of filthy shit I'd never allow myself to utter if it weren't for the words I'm trying desperately to hold back.

But Valencia is undaunted. She moans and sighs, and responds with her own dirty talk. Yes, I make her feel good, and yes, she can't wait for me to shoot my load in her ass. Her words: *shoot your load*. When I ask if she's a dirty girl and she says, "Only for *you*," I nearly explode right then and there.

Finally, we agree she's ready. I lube up my cock and position it at her rear entrance. She breathes through the stretch, and when I finally sink inside, it's the most incredible thing I've ever felt. Tight, and hot, and *trusting*.

God, she fucking *trusts* me.

Last night, with the blindfold, it felt like she did, but hearing her say it, while doing *this* . . . it floors me.

Her trust makes it easy to be gentle, but when she demands more, my control snaps. Her mewling cries spur me on as I pound into her, but it's not enough. I need to see her face.

I pull out and flip her onto her back.

"Hold these," I growl, shoving her knees up. I'm absolutely feral with the need to make her come.

She complies, spreading herself wide. I pour more lube over both of us, dimly grateful that she laid towels on the bed before we began. But then I'm pushing into her again, and I can't think about anything else but our bodies. I plant one hand on her belly, swirling circles over her clit with my thumb while I pump into her. Everything is hot and intense and wet and *fuck, she feels so good*, but then she's shouting—

"Gideon, I'm coming!"

And she *does*.

And then *I* do, rutting like an animal while fire races through my veins, magnified by the plug in my ass. I spurt inside her, then fall to my knees to watch it dripping out of her.

Or maybe my legs buckled. I can't tell.

I'm breathing hard, the way I do after outracing my demons on the treadmill. But my mind is at peace in a way I've never felt before.

"Are you okay?" My throat feels raw. She's blinking dazedly at the ceiling but shifts her gaze to focus on me.

"I . . ." She clears her throat. "I think I had an out-of-body experience."

I huff out a weary laugh. "I think I did, too."

"Does it . . . ?" Her question is slow and uncertain. "Does anal always feels like that, or was this . . . ?"

The thought goes unfinished, but I know what she means. Was this special? Was this just *us*?

"It doesn't always feel like that." There's gravel in my voice, like this is a confession, or a declaration.

Maybe she has some inkling of that, because she doesn't say anything else, until, "Come here."

My limbs feel heavy as I climb onto the bed. She helps me remove my plug, then cuddles against my side with her head on my chest.

Me? I still can't catch my breath. This woman is the stuff of dreams. But she's *real*. Real, and right here with me.

For three more days.

I put that out of my mind, because as explosive as tonight has been, there's something I'm looking forward to even more.

Sleeping with Valencia in my bed.

We shower together, then slide under the covers, naked, warm, and drowsy. I curl around her and press my face into her neck, breathing the scent of her coconut shampoo deep into my lungs.

It's *heaven*.

"Good night, Gideon," she whispers.

And for the first time all year, I fall asleep immediately.

Chapter 16

Gideon

Day 10: Sensual Massage & Christmas Movies

When I wake with my arms wrapped around Valencia and her hair in my face, it's the most rested I've felt in a long time. We eat gingerbread cookies for breakfast and add a splash of coquito to our coffee and tea. Then we engage in a little midmorning sensual massage, which culminates in easy, languid lovemaking. It's different from yesterday, but just as perfect. I hold her for a long time afterward.

After we clean up, I pull out two pairs of matching red and green plaid pajamas—necessary attire for a lazy morning watching classic Christmas movies. I don't think I imagine that Valencia is a little misty-eyed when we put them on.

We can't decide what to watch, so we write movie titles on slips of paper and toss them into a mixing bowl. Valencia selects one with a flourish.

Home Alone.

We snuggle on my big leather sofa with our feet resting on the coffee table and the fireplace flickering merrily under the wall-mounted flat-screen TV. Valencia falls asleep halfway through the movie with her head on my shoulder, drooling a little on my pajama shirt. I'm hit with a pang of contentment so pervasive it makes my chest ache.

I look around my apartment, taking in the massive tree decorated with blinking white lights, a mixed assortment of garlands, and glass ornaments. There's a red velvet runner across the coffee table, a wreath hanging on the apartment door, and a sprig of mistletoe over the kitchen doorway. Every time we pass under it, we stop and kiss.

Valencia's brought so much into my life. Color and sparkle, sweetness and spice, companionship and cuddles. She's brightened my world, the way the trappings of the holiday season, commercial though they may be, enliven the darkest and coldest time of the year. What the hell am I going to do without her, when all I have left in front of me are the cold gray days of winter in New York?

The truth is, I've never wanted anything more than I want to be with her. To have her here, in my arms and in my home, for the rest of this month and all the months—years?—that come after.

But what does *she* want?

Does she want *me*?

My phone buzzes with an incoming call. It's my mother. She's arriving in two days, so I should answer.

Carefully, I slide out from under the blanket and position Valencia so she's lying down. She makes an adorable hum and curls up in the warm spot I've vacated. I smile down at her for a second, then stride into my bedroom to accept the call.

"Mom?"

"Bonjour, mon amour."

I switch to French. "Tout va bien?"

"Oui, oui," she says airily, and then her tone changes. "However, there is a change of plans. You will come here for Christmas. To Paris."

I halt my pacing. "But you're supposed to come to New York."

"Ah, Gideon. It's so much better here. Take a flight tomorrow and come join me."

Tomorrow? I have two days left with Valencia. "Mom, I can't leave yet."

"Are you working?"

"No, but—"

"Then come to Paris." She says it as if it's as simple as running to the store for a carton of milk.

"I have plans," I blurt out. "On Christmas Eve."

Her tone sharpens ever so slightly. "Well, cancel them and come see your mother."

I pinch the bridge of my nose. "I have to go, Mom. I'll call you later."

"Send me your flight information."

There's no mistaking the snap of command in her words. I say goodbye and hang up.

I let out a long sigh and trudge back to the living room. I hear Valencia's voice, and when I round the corner, I see she's on the phone.

"That's so nice of you, Heather. I would love to see you and Patrick, and, of course, Fern, but . . ."

At the mention of Fern, I realize what's happening. If Heather and Patrick are Fern's parents, that also makes them . . .

No fucking way.

I stalk over, letting my stockinged feet slam on the floor so Valencia hears me coming. She sends me a weary look but continues speaking to Heather Mulholland.

"Yes, I always enjoyed spending Christmas morning with you, but I don't think it would be . . . All right, maybe Christmas Eve dinner . . ."

My jaw tightens and I shake my head.

Valencia gives a helpless shrug. "Well, if you think it'll be okay, maybe I can stop by for a little bit."

I run my hands through my hair and fight back a growl.

"Sure, Heather. Thank you. See you then. Bye."

When she hangs up, I let loose. "What the hell was that?" Lingering frustration from the call with my own mother makes my voice harsher than I intend.

"Gideon, please." Valencia doesn't meet my eyes as she pulls the blanket around her.

"Should I guess? Because it sounded like you were letting Mulholland's mother steamroll you into spending Christmas with your *ex-fiancé*."

Her eyes squeeze shut, and my heart sinks. Shit, I've gone too far. But when she opens her eyes again, they're blazing with dark fire.

"Do you think I don't realize that?" she hisses. "But that woman is the closest thing I've had to a parent for *years*. I miss her. And besides that, she's not easy to say no to. She wanted me to come over for Christmas Day, and this is the compromise."

I glare at her. "You and I already have plans."

"It gets dark at four o'clock. We can go see the lights before dinner, and then your obligation to me will be over and you'll be free to spend the rest of the day with your mom."

The word *obligation* pings my radar. This isn't the first time she's said it. But I don't want to tell her my mother is staying in Paris, so I ignore it and try a different tack.

"I'll go with you."

She chokes out a disbelieving laugh. "Are you kidding? You and Everett, in the same room? With *me*? I don't think so."

It does sound like a recipe for disaster, but the thought of her being around him makes my blood boil. I don't know what happened between them, only that Valencia broke off the engagement, but I wouldn't put it past that dickhead to try to cajole his way back into her life. That's how he was in school, always worming his way into and out of trouble. I don't know what the hell she ever saw in him, but then, I don't know what she sees in *me*, either.

I press the issue. "You shouldn't have to go alone. That was our deal, right? To keep each other company leading up to Christmas."

She tries to shrug that off, but I can see it gets to her. "Fern will be there, and her parents. And probably some of their friends and relatives."

"That's not going to be weird for you? With everyone knowing you're his ex?"

"Of *course* it'll be weird!" The words burst out of her, tinged with exasperation, and—*shit*—sadness. "But they're the closest thing to family I have left."

What about me? I think, but it's ridiculous. I have no right to say that.

Her shoulders slump and she rubs the back of her neck. "Look, can we just give it a rest and finish the movie? We were having a really nice day before this call."

I don't want to give it a rest. I love arguing, and I love *winning* arguments even more. But this isn't a case, and Valencia isn't the opposing counsel. I can tell this conversation is hurting her, and that's the last thing I want to do.

So I sink onto the couch beside her, and I don't mention my mother's directive that I drop everything and fly to Paris.

Because I've already decided. There's no way I'm abandoning Valencia. Not now. Not ever, if I can help it.

I cup her face in my hands, kissing her with lazy strokes of my tongue until the tension seeps out of her and she melts against my chest.

With our foreheads touching, I whisper into the scant space between us. "Better?"

"Much. Thank you."

"Anytime." I mean it with every fiber of my being.

We finish the movie and put on the sequel, and eat so much gingerbread we feel sick.

But in the back of my mind, I can't stop thinking about how our twelve-day adventure is coming to an end.

And how desperate I am for it to continue.

So I come to another conclusion. I am not going to Paris, but I *am* accompanying Valencia to the Mulhollands' for Christmas Eve.

Whether she likes it or not.

Chapter 17

Valencia

Day 11: Mutual Masturbation & Miniature Trains

Despite our argument, my weekend with Gideon is amazing. Anal was . . . I hesitate to say *transcendent*, because that sounds hyperbolic, so let's just say it was *really fucking good*. Also . . . surprisingly emotional.

Since neither of us have work the next day, I spend Sunday night at his place, too. I fall asleep nestled securely in his arms, but when I wake on Monday morning, a ball of dread settles into my gut.

Tomorrow is Christmas Eve.

Our list is almost done, and the thought of not seeing him every day already has me feeling bereft.

Look, I know I'm a lot. When Gideon suggested we do holiday shit together, he probably thought it would be one or two activities. I planned *twelve*—twenty-four, if you count all the sexy prompts, too. A lot of people might have bailed, or only wanted to do the sex stuff. Gideon, however, has not only indulged, but *expanded upon* every silly whim I've thrown his way.

Like the banned-book ornaments. Or buying six vibrators. Or decorating his bedroom to look like the *North Fucking Pole*.

But then he had to go and get us matching Christmas pajamas, and that, somehow, was the thing that broke me.

Part of me wishes he'd stop being so considerate, because it's just going to make it harder to say goodbye. The other part wants to build a blanket fort on his ridiculous leather couch and move in.

But the end of the list isn't the only thing weighing on me.

The moment we complete our final outing in Dyker Heights, Brooklyn, where the residents go all out with Christmas lights, I'll be on my way to Christmas Eve dinner with the Mulhollands.

Including Everett.

Talk about emotional whiplash.

Still, I'm determined not to let an anxiety spiral or thoughts of my ex ruin my morning. Not when mutual masturbation is on the menu.

When Gideon and I made the list, we went back and forth about this prompt. Would we be bringing each other to orgasm, or doing it solo at the same time? The thought of watching Gideon jerk himself off was too enticing to pass up, so I insisted on the latter.

And oh, man, was that the right choice.

I recline on his bed, propped up on pillows, my hand between my legs. He's across the room in a plush armchair, fully naked, stroking his lubed cock with strong, sure pulls. Everything about him, from his lean runner's build to his big hands to his heavy erection and tight balls, makes me hot.

And God, the *mouth* on this man. Gideon coaches me through two orgasms, delivering a soliloquy of praise, requests, commands, and fantasies. I'm trembling and sweaty by the time he comes, pumping his fist faster before spilling over his hand and onto the floor.

The reckless abandon on his face, the tightening of his muscles, the way his eyes never leave mine—it's super sexy but also fills me with an aching tenderness.

This doesn't just feel like a holiday hookup.

And maybe it never did.

That thought elicits a different sort of trembling as Gideon cleans himself off and joins me on the bed. Draping himself over me, he nuzzles his face into my hair.

"So soft," he murmurs. "So pretty." He twines the curls around his fingers one by one.

I close my eyes, and instead of worrying about tomorrow, I let myself enjoy his warm weight on me and the delicate tugs on my scalp.

Gideon has apologized repeatedly for every bad thing he ever said about my hair, which is why I now feel comfortable enough to let him see it in its natural state—and he's *obsessed*. Still, I'm planning to flat-iron it before we go to the Bronx for the New York Botanical Garden's Holiday Train Show, and I'd rather do that at home with my full collection of hair products. So after I nudge him off me, we take a shower—with one more quickie for the road—and head to my apartment.

I'm coming out of the bedroom with my hair sleek and smooth, like a Latina Morticia Addams, when I hear Gideon's voice. At first I think he's talking to Archie, but he sounds angry, and it takes a few seconds to realize he's speaking French.

"No, Mom. Je te l'ai dit, je ne vais pas à Paris pour Christmas."

I freeze. He's talking to his mother. And even my basic French can decipher his statement.

I told you, I'm not going to Paris for Christmas.

My stomach lurches. On that first night we spent together, he told me his mother was in France and that she'd be coming back to New York on Christmas Eve.

Apparently, something changed.

And he didn't tell me.

I play hopscotch over the creaky floorboards as I tiptoe toward the kitchen, where Gideon is unpacking the sushi we ordered for lunch. The phone is pressed between his ear and his shoulder, and Archie is winding around his ankles, meowing for food. Gideon continues to argue with his mother in French.

Why wouldn't he go? Could it be . . . for me?

The thought makes me cold. I'm torn between selfishly wanting him to stay and a pang of grief. He still has one parent left, and she's grieving, too; he should spend the holidays with her.

He breaks off mid-sentence and lets out a frustrated huff. I suspect his mom hung up.

He doesn't know I'm here, and I take a moment to watch him. He sets the phone down and braces his hands on the kitchen counter. His head falls forward and his shoulders hunch like he's carrying the weight of the world.

Or maybe just the weight of his own world. His mother . . . and me. Opposing responsibilities.

The last thing I ever wanted was to be a burden.

"Go to France." I speak quietly, but he still jolts. When he spins around, his expression is a mixture of alarm and guilt. He stares at me for a beat.

"You speak French."

It's not a question, but I nod anyway. "I took it for three years in high school."

"Shit." He sags against the counter. "I forgot."

It was one of the few classes we didn't share. Since both of my parents spoke Spanish and I'm semifluent, I'd taken French. Gideon had taken Spanish, although I forgot it was because *he's* fluent in French.

"Gideon, you have to go." He shakes his head, but I barrel on before he can argue with me. "The list is just a silly thing we made up. I'll be fine."

He scowls at me. "It's not silly."

"Well, it doesn't constitute a binding contract. You're perfectly free to end it early."

"No. We have an agreement. Effective until Christmas Eve."

He sounds so stubborn that I scoff. "Are you going to sue me for breach of contract?"

"I'm simply reminding you that we have a *deal*." The words press through gritted teeth.

I toss my newly straightened hair over one shoulder and try to sound flippant. "I'm letting you out of it."

"Valencia, I don't *want* to get out of it."

"You should. Why stay in New York alone when you could be in Paris with your mother?"

"I won't *be* alone."

The unspoken words hang in the air between us: *I'll be with you.*

But I can't let him do this for me. And I can't have him feeling guilty for abandoning me. That's taking things too far.

"The list ends tomorrow night, remember? We never agreed to spend Christmas Day together."

His eyes blaze. "Then we'll *renegotiate the fucking terms.*"

I hug myself and turn away. "I'm too tired to argue. Go to France, Gideon."

"Only if you come with me."

"What?" That brings me up short, and I stare at him.

He's regained his composure, and he's wearing what must be his lawyer face. I know, because it looks a lot like mine—tight jaw, firm lips, brow smooth but somehow menacing. It's his eyes that change the most, though. They're impenetrable, like a wall of ice.

I attempt to chip away at it. "I can't fuck off to France with you."

"Do you have a passport?" he asks calmly. "I'll buy your ticket right now."

Lord. I can't let this man buy me an international plane ticket, probably first class, within a week and a half of reuniting with him. Even if the fact that he offered without a second thought gives me a thrill.

"No, Gideon. Anyway, I'm expected at the Mulhollands' for dinner tomorrow."

His expression darkens. "Valencia, I will be *damned* if you visit your ex for Christmas without me."

"And I'm not going to let you miss the holidays with your one remaining parent because of *me*!" The words are torn from my throat with more force than I'd intended, but I can't stop. "If you knew what I would give to have one more Christmas with mine . . ." I cut off that thought, shaking my head vehemently. "I can't let you make that kind of sacrifice for me. I *won't*. Consider our agreement terminated, effective immediately."

"Valencia—"

"Leave it alone, Noble!"

My words crack like a whip, and he stills. All emotion drains from his face, leaving his eyes the cold, hard jade I remember from our youth.

"Are we back to that, Torres?" His voice is chilly, with a slight emphasis on my last name. It's completely at odds with the heartfelt yearning I heard a second ago when he said my first.

I've hurt him. I didn't want to, but I don't know how else to do this.

"Go to France," I say for the third time, and my voice cracks a little. "*Please*, Gideon. Just . . . go. Now."

He stares at me for a long time, but I can't meet his gaze. Finally, he sighs. In three long strides, he's past me and yanking his coat off the hook by my apartment door.

And then he's gone.

I slump into a chair at my dining table, blinking at the little Christmas tree covered in ornaments he bought for me. The lights blur as my eyes fill with tears, and I think about the red envelope I slipped into his stocking just this morning.

When I hear the front door of the building slam, I pillow my head on my arms and cry.

Chapter 18

GIDEON

Christmas Eve
Day 12: Dinner with the Mulhollands

If Valencia thinks I'm leaving her alone for Christmas, she's out of her fucking mind.

I walk back to my apartment, letting the brisk December air cool my temper. I get what she's doing, and why, but it doesn't matter. I won't abandon her.

I'm . . . in love with her.

Which is what I *should* have said instead of all that *agreement* and *deal* crap. And maybe I would have if she hadn't caught me off guard.

Truth is, she's been catching me off guard since I spotted her in the club.

As I walk, I formulate a plan. Pulling out my phone, I open one of my rarely used social media apps and do a user search. Then I send a private message.

Two seconds later, a reply pops up.

What do you want, Knobble?

I grin. *Bingo.*

The next evening is Christmas Eve, and I'm waiting in front of the ornate limestone exterior of the Mulhollands' Park Avenue apartment building when Valencia arrives on foot.

Her expression goes flat when she sees me.

"What are you doing here, Gideon?"

"Oh, we're back to first names?" I shouldn't fuck with her, but I can't help it. When she called me Noble yesterday, she might as well have eviscerated me with a candy cane.

She sends me an exasperated look, but she doesn't object when I fall into step beside her and enter the building.

The doorman recognizes her and they exchange season's greetings before we get on the elevator. I'm once again reminded that she must have spent a lot of time here while she was dating, and then engaged to, Mulholland.

"Do *not* make a scene," she hisses at me once the elevator doors shut and we begin our ascent.

"I won't if he doesn't."

She heaves a sigh and casts her gaze toward the ceiling. Then she glances at me from the corner of her eye. "Should I take this to mean you're not going to France?"

"As I told you *and* my mother, no, I am not going to Paris. I'm staying right here and celebrating Christmas in New York"—I glare at her—"with *you.*"

The tension in her face eases, and she seems to be on the verge of smiling when the elevator doors open. When we approach the Mulhollands' door and knock, it's opened almost immediately by Fern. Delicious scents waft toward us, but Fern shoots a look over her shoulder and steps out, shutting the door partway behind her.

"Merry Christmas, Happy Hanukkah, et cetera, et cetera." She plants a smacking kiss on Valencia's cheek, then grabs the collar of my coat and pulls me down to do the same. When she releases me, she turns back to Valencia and winces. "Ev's not here yet. I warned him that you were bringing a date, but I didn't tell him who."

Valencia shoots me an accusatory glare. "I didn't realize I was bringing him, either, or that you two are partners in crime."

Fern's tone is utterly unrepentant. "Look, babe, I'm chaotic-neutral at best, and my brother has been a little dipshit this year. He has it coming. I just wanted to warn *you*"—she makes finger guns at me—"that Ev is a professional hockey player, and he's kinda free with his fists."

I clench my jaw. I'm not a fighter, never needed to be, but I'd make an exception here. Out loud I say, "I'm not worried."

Valencia covers her face with both hands. "Fucking hell."

"Should we get this party started?" Fern's smile is a little too gleeful, but when she opens the door, we follow her in.

I've never been here, since Mulholland and I weren't friends, but I lived only a few blocks away on Fifth Avenue, right across from the Met. Despite being in the same neighborhood, though, our childhood homes couldn't be more different. This apartment is big and warm and colorful, bursting with people, music, and enough mismatched furniture to give my mother the vapors.

"Valencia, honey!" A short woman with caramel-blond highlights who looks like a Gen X version of Fern charges toward us. She envelopes Valencia in a big hug, and it's suddenly obvious why we're here. Maybe things didn't work out with the son, but Mulholland's mom cares about Valencia and clearly misses her.

Then Mrs. Mulholland turns to me, and her expression is one of stunned recognition. "Oh, my goodness, you're Andrea Noble's boy! Look how tall you've gotten. Remind me of your name, dear. Is it Gabriel?"

"Gideon." I lean down to let her hug me, too, and something about this whole interaction makes me wish my own mother were here in New York, even though she'd call this level of effusiveness gauche. "Thank you for having us, Mrs. Mulholland. Merry Christmas."

At my side, Valencia stiffens at the "us," and I don't miss the way Mrs. Mulholland's eyes dart from her to me. But all she says is, "Please, call me Heather."

There is apparently a whole crew of Mulhollands, and I'm introduced to the father—a stocky, balding man named Patrick—a pair of uncles, their wives, and too many cousins to count. Fern stands apart with a glass of eggnog, watching the proceedings with an anticipatory gleam in her eyes.

No one mentions Everett Mulholland.

Once we've made the rounds—and Valencia has handed Heather a bottle of homemade coquito—I pull Valencia into a quiet corner of the living room. "I need to tell you something."

"Are you doing okay?" She sends me a concerned look.

"Fine. Are you?"

She gives a little shrug. "Could be worse. What did you want to talk about?"

I take her hands and sweep my gaze over her slowly. "I just wanted to tell you how beautiful you look tonight."

Her lips part in a bashful grin, and her cheeks turn an endearing shade of pink. She's wearing a long-sleeved black shirt tucked into a flared, red and black plaid skirt that hits below her knee. It's tasteful and casual, but still stunning.

Then again, I think she's gorgeous in a T-shirt and sweatpants.

"You didn't need to say that, but thank you."

"I wanted to say it," I insist. "Just like I want to tell you how fucking strong you are for even entertaining the idea of coming here. You have a kind heart, Valencia Torres. Kinder than any of us deserve."

Her eyes go soft and dewy, and she opens her mouth to speak. But before she can respond, there's a commotion at the door.

Mulholland has arrived.

"Merry Xmas, fam!" he shouts, louder than is appropriate for an indoor holiday gathering.

And yes, he really says "Xmas."

Then his face transforms into a ferocious scowl as he spots Valencia and me holding hands.

"What the fuck is *he* doing here?" He roars it, and his mother is on his ass in a second, telling him to shut up, but her words have no effect.

Mulholland storms over. He's big—not as tall as I am but built like the professional athlete he is, with hands the size of dinner plates. Otherwise, he's regular-looking with sleepy eyes, short brown hair, a ruddy complexion, and an overlarge nose that's clearly been broken since the last time I saw him.

I don't want to fight with this guy in his mother's living room, but I'm also not letting him get through me to Valencia. I step in front of her, but she, of course, has other plans, and steps in front of *me*.

"Him?" Mulholland sounds apoplectic as he jabs a finger in my direction. Everyone in the room tenses, but I don't flinch. "This is your date? Gideon Fucking Noble?"

"Everett!" Heather shrieks from the kitchen doorway. "Watch your mouth."

Mulholland ignores her, but when Valencia snaps, "Lower your voice," he seems to calm somewhat. He reaches for her, so *I* reach for *him*, but Valencia neatly sidesteps his touch and blocks me from grabbing him.

"Whatever you have to say to me, Everett, you can do it in private." Her tone is prim and professional, and I can suddenly imagine her in court.

"Fine." He appears to be grinding his teeth as he stomps down a hallway with Valencia two paces behind him.

It takes every ounce of my self-control—and Fern's hand on my arm—to keep from following them.

Fern watches them go, her brow pinched. "They need to have it out. This has been a long time coming."

I grunt. "Does it have to be now?"

She sighs. "Now or never."

But despite leaving the room, their voices carry. Mulholland seems incapable of speaking in a normal volume, something I vaguely remember from school. Valencia's voice is strained but louder than usual.

"What the fuck, V? You used to hate that guy."

"I never *hated* him, and that was a long time—"

"So, what? Is he your new boyfriend?"

"I'm . . . I'm seeing him."

"*Seeing* him?" Mulholland's voice drips with scornful disbelief. "Fucking him, you mean."

All the assembled relatives suck in a collective breath, but before anyone can speak, there's the sound of a slap. I lunge for the hall but Fern grabs me and yanks me back. Mr. Mulholland—Patrick—is already on his way.

Mulholland sounds flabbergasted. "I can't believe you smacked me!"

"You deserved it." Valencia's reply is angrier than I've ever heard her. "Who I *fuck* is none of your goddamned business."

"It is when you fuck him in *my* apartment and bring him to *my* parents' house!"

Patrick barks, "Apologize to her, *now*."

But it's Valencia's voice that comes through loud and clear. "Fuck you, Everett. I gave you nine years of my life, and what did you do? You cheated on me and then said it was *my* fault.

You have *no* say in what I do with my life, who I do it with, or where."

There's a gasp, and I see Heather clutching the front of her ugly Christmas sweater. I guess the cheating thing wasn't common knowledge. I certainly didn't know.

It makes me hate the guy even more.

Next to me, Fern knocks a phone out of her teenage cousin's hand. "If you live stream this, I will end you."

There's a pause from the hallway, and Mulholland's voice borders on contrite. "Look, V—"

"No, you don't get to say anything else to me." Valencia's words cut like a knife. "I'd hoped we could be civil for the sake of your family, whom I love very much, but apparently I was wrong. Goodbye, Everett. And go to hell!"

I want to applaud. That's the love of my life, standing up for herself and telling that jerkwad where to stick it, but when Valencia reappears with tears streaming down her face, everything in me goes cold.

"I'm sorry, everyone." She dashes at her eyes. "I never meant for . . ."

Heather is at her side in an instant, and I'm only a second behind her. I'm vibrating with the need to take Valencia in my arms and spirit her away, but Heather is embracing her, and I don't want to interrupt.

"Don't apologize, honey. You're family. And sometimes families have ups and downs." Heather pulls back to look Valencia in the eye. "I'll always be here for you. You know that, don't you?"

"It's really nice to hear it." Valencia's whisper is high and tight. She's holding on by a thread. I have to get her out of here.

I'm already stepping forward when Heather turns to me. "Take care of her, won't you?"

I nod solemnly. "I will, ma'am."

Fern is waiting at the door with our coats. We're on our way out when Mulholland reappears, his cheek red and his mouth twisted in anger.

"One more month, V," he shouts. "And then you better get your skank ass out of my apartment!"

I turn right back around, fists clenched, but two Mulholland cousins grab me by the arms. A red haze clouds my vision, and I'm barely aware of Fern shoving at my chest or Heather Mulholland screaming at her son.

"Don't do this," Fern hisses. "Valencia needs you now."

That gets through to me like nothing else could. Without a word, I swing back to Valencia and usher her into the hallway with an arm around her shoulders.

Fern follows us out, her expression full of regret.

"I'm so sorry, Valencia." Fern pulls her into a hug. "Part of me knew there was a chance he'd punch Knobble here in his pretty face, but I never thought Ev would be like that to *you*."

"He's always had a temper." Valencia says this with hollow resignation, and Fern and I exchange a concerned glance. This little display has provided some alarming insight into Valencia and Mulholland's past relationship.

"You'll never have to see him again," Fern promises. "I'll make sure of it."

The elevator arrives and Fern passes me a tote bag, which appears to be full of hastily packed food. We murmur our goodbyes to Fern and step on. The second the doors close, I haul Valencia into my arms and hug her with everything I have.

"I'm so fucking proud of you," I grit out, kissing the top of her head. "But you didn't deserve to be spoken to that way. Please tell me you know that."

She lets out a shuddering breath and sags against me. I'm all but holding her up.

"I'm glad you're here," she whispers. "I'm really glad you're here."

"I'll always be here for you," I say, but this isn't the place for grand declarations, so I order a car to bring us back to my apartment, where I can bare my soul to her in privacy.

Chapter 19

VALENCIA

We don't speak in the car, but Gideon holds my hand the whole way from the Upper East Side to Chelsea, stroking my knuckles gently with his thumb. Focusing on that simple, repetitive motion helps me process what just happened.

God, I can't believe I *slapped* Everett. But after years of remaining calm and rational during his explosive tantrums, I'd fucking had it. Maybe now his family can stop wondering why we broke up. And while my relationship with his mother might never be the same, I'm grateful that I haven't lost her completely.

The tears have stopped by the time Gideon bustles me into his apartment. I think he would have carried me from the car to the door if he thought I'd let him, but I'm okay. Really.

Well, sort of. And only because Gideon is here.

He hangs up my coat, then peers into the bag Fern pressed on him.

"What's that?" My voice comes out raspy.

"Looks like dinner." He puts the bag in the kitchen, then comes back and cups my face. A line appears between his brows. "Tell me what you need right now, Valencia."

I fist my hands in his sage green sweater and tug him closer. "You. I need *you*."

He searches my face for a long moment. "Yeah?"

"Yeah."

He does pick me up then, and I attack his mouth with soft, nipping kisses as he carries me to his bedroom. Somehow, he seems to know I need to be in control tonight, and after we shed our clothes, he maneuvers me so I'm on top. With his hands on my hips urging me on, I ride him until I can't see straight.

And it is *exactly* what I need.

When it's over, I collapse by his side in a tangle of bedding.

"Ready to talk?" he asks.

I let out a winded laugh. "Right now?"

"Maybe in a couple minutes."

My thighs are sticky, but I'm not ready to leave this bed. And before we discuss what happened tonight, there's something important I want to say.

"Thank you for coming with me. And for staying. In the city, I mean. I didn't want you to, but . . . I'm really happy you're here."

Gideon threads his fingers through the ends of my hair, and his eyes glitter with a fathomless wealth of emotion. "I couldn't leave you."

"Because of the list?" I say it lightly, not daring to hope his reasoning runs deeper than that.

He shakes his head slowly, his eyes never leaving mine. "Not because of the list."

My insides quake like I'm standing at the edge of a precipice, and I'm terrified there won't be anything—any*one*— to catch me if I fall. Still, I ask, "Then why?"

"Come on, Valencia." His tone is chiding. "You know why."

I let out a shuddering breath. "I've had a rough couple of days. Maybe you'd better spell it out."

He gazes at me for so long my pulse skyrockets again.

Finally, he speaks. "I couldn't leave you, because . . . I love you."

Everything in me stills.

"You do?" My voice comes out small and uncertain. Hopeful.

He nods.

"Are you sure?"

"Valencia." His voice is utterly calm. "Where's your overnight bag?"

I glance over the side of the bed, where I left a large tote bag the day before. It's not there.

"Top drawer, on the right."

I squint at the dresser. I'm sure he doesn't mean what I think he means, but I climb off the bed and open the drawer.

Sure enough, my spare clothes are neatly folded alongside his crisp white undershirts.

I clear my throat. "And my toiletries?"

"Bathroom. First drawer on the left. That entire sink area is yours."

My heart races. Something is happening, but I'm too afraid to name it.

Except . . . we agreed to communicate, right? I can just *ask* him.

I shut the drawer carefully. "What does this mean, Gideon?"

He leaves the bed and comes over to me. We're still naked, and I'm momentarily distracted by the shift of his muscles as he walks. Suddenly, he's right in front of me, brushing a lock of hair over my ear.

"It means . . ." He bites that captivating lower lip, and his tone turns wry. "That I'm writing a eulogy for my leather sofa."

I blink, pulling my gaze from his mouth to his eyes. "What? Why?"

He grimaces. "I've seen what your cat did to yours."

"My—my cat? Archimedes?"

"Do you have another cat who's been hiding this whole time?"

"No, but . . ." My mind goes blank. All I can do is glance back at the dresser.

Gideon touches my chin, gently turning me to face him again.

"That drawer is just the beginning, love. I'd like it if you—and Archie, of course—would move in with me."

"Oh." The trembling is back. "That's . . . a lot more than a spare toothbrush."

"I know." He rubs the back of his neck and looks almost embarrassed. "Initially, that's all I was going to ask because I didn't think I deserved more, and even that would've made me happier than you could possibly imagine. But I want you to know where I stand, Valencia. Twelve days with you isn't enough. Honestly, I'm not sure forever will be enough. Maybe that's over the top, but . . ." He shrugs, his lips curving in a sheepish smile. "That's me."

A week ago, I would've laughed and called him a drama queen. But I know he's serious. And too much has happened for me to hide behind humor, the way I did at Rolf's.

Even as my heart begs me to accept what he's saying, that old fear of being a burden rises up, and I need to know that this is not because he thinks I'm a victim.

I swallow down the lump in my throat. "Is this because of what happened today?"

He looks so taken aback, I already know it's not. "You think I'm asking you to move in with me out of—what? Pity? Obligation?"

Anguish squeezes my voice. *"Yes."*

"Valencia, I unpacked your bag yesterday after I got home."

I quickly review the timeline. "After our argument? Weren't you angry?"

He waves that away. "'Go to France' is hardly the worst thing you've ever said to me. I just want you to see that I'm serious about you. About *us*."

"But what about when the holidays are over? I've enjoyed every second we've spent together, but things won't be the same once I go back to work."

His lips quirk in amusement. "Valencia, I already know that you're mission driven and hardworking. Besides, those aren't *bad* qualities."

I swallow. "It's been a problem. Before."

His expression darkens, but all he says is, "It's not a problem to *me*."

And with that, something becomes startlingly clear. All year, I've believed that my commitment to my job would hinder a new relationship. That even though Everett cheated, I was also partly to blame.

But Everett never understood this fundamental part of me. He just wanted me to be the perfect WAG and make him look good.

Gideon might have teased me when we were kids, but since we've reunited, he's respected me and my decisions. It couldn't have been easy for him to stand back while I spoke with Everett, but Gideon didn't try to stop me. Instead, he supported my choice and comforted me afterward. And even when I didn't want him to, he put *me* first, rather than letting me suffer through a painful situation alone.

That's love. Standing by my side while I do hard things, being a safe space to share my thoughts and feelings, and enthusiastically participating in a silly, sexy Christmas list, just to make me happy.

I think of the sealed red envelope I hid in his stocking. Maybe we really are on the same page.

"I'm scared," I confess, because even that's easy to say to him. "This is going really fast."

"It scares me a little, too." His smile is tender. "But that just means we care about doing this right. And besides, we have a secret weapon."

"We do?"

His grin widens. "Open communication."

He's right. Maybe it's only been twelve days, but we've created a solid foundation. I don't know if I'd be brave enough to build upon it myself, but Gideon has already shown he's along for the ride, no matter how ridiculous my ideas might be, and he's willing to put his heart on the line.

How can I do anything less?

I tilt my face to his. "Say it again?"

Warmth suffuses his features. He knows exactly what I mean.

"I love you, Valencia."

Tears spring to my eyes. I throw my arms around his neck, and he lifts me until I'm on tiptoe, our bodies flush together.

In his embrace, I finally find the courage to name the emotion I've been subduing. "I love you, too," I whisper into his neck.

He exhales, and it's like his entire being relaxes. "Thank fuck." He pulls back and gives me a relieved smile. "I didn't know what I was going to do if you responded any differently."

I choke out a watery laugh. "This feels way too soon. But it also feels . . . right?"

"It feels *inevitable*." His fervent declaration ends with a kiss that has me dragging him back to the bed.

After a quick fuck and an even quicker shower, we heat up the food and sit side by side at the dining table in our matching pajamas.

"Did you really enlist Fern's help?" I ask, piling slices of ham and various side dishes onto my plate.

"I just messaged her for the address."

I swallow a bite of mashed potatoes. "I'm surprised she didn't tell you to go fuck yourself."

Gideon's cheeks redden and he becomes very interested in his green beans. "She did, actually. And I was forced to admit that I'm in love with you."

I slap the table in mock outrage. "You told her before you told me?"

He raises a sardonic eyebrow. "Only because you demanded I leave."

"I'm sorry." I reach over and take his hand. "My reaction was more about me missing my parents and not wanting to burden you."

He gives my fingers a squeeze. "If I'd had the courage then to tell you how I felt, maybe you would've seen why it was such an easy decision for me to make."

"I might not have believed you," I muse. "But I can't imagine why you would've put yourself through all that drama today for any other reason."

"So you believe me? That I love you?" Vulnerability shines in his eyes, and I nod.

"Good." His tone turns brisk. "Then you'll understand why I'm hiring a moving company tomorrow to get you out of that prick's apartment."

"Tomorrow is Christmas Day."

"Fine. I'll wait a day. But you're not sleeping there again."

I sigh at his high-handedness. "Gideon—"

"Please don't debate me on this." He's wearing his lawyer face, which means he's digging his heels in. "He screamed at you and called you names with his entire family present. And I've seen the fights he's gotten into on the ice. Forgive me if I'm not comfortable with you being there while he still has keys."

Because it's exactly the sort of advice I would give to someone in my situation, I don't argue. "Okay, but I'll find a new place as soon as—"

"Oh, my God, Valencia." Gideon plunks his elbows on the table and drops his head into his hands. "What part of me telling you that I want you *and your cat* to move in did you not understand?"

"I didn't think you meant in two days!"

He raises his head and pins me with a look. "I don't."

"Oh, then—"

"I meant *today*."

I stare at him blankly. "Oh."

His expression softens. "Look, if you really don't want to move in yet, or at all, I'll help you find another option. Because as much as I want to fall asleep with you every night and wake up next to you every morning, the most important thing to me is your safety. Just tell me what you want, Valencia, and I'll do it. I'll do *anything* for you."

I swallow hard, struck speechless by the earnestness of his words.

This has gone extremely fast, and I'm not usually the type to rush into things. Unfortunately, that means I haven't rushed *out* of things, either.

I stayed in my last relationship far longer than I should have. Even before Everett cheated, I knew we weren't a good fit. But I said yes when he proposed because it seemed like that was the path we were on.

The night I saw Gideon, I stepped off the beaten path of the workaholic bookworm and onto a new one with him. I'm eager to see where it leads. And if he's willing to have me and my cat and all my books cluttering up his beautiful apartment, well . . .

Why wait?

I consider asking how he'll feel about making a "New Year, New Home" list, but I already know what his answer will be.

"Okay," I say quietly. "I'm in."

His fork clatters as he pulls me into his arms.

Chapter 20

GIDEON

Christmas Day
Day 13: Bondage & Volunteering

Valencia wakes me on Christmas morning with a soft kiss. "Feliz Navidad, mi amor."

Happiness washes through me when I see her sitting up in bed next to me. "Joyeux Noël, mon coeur." But then I notice her devious expression. She holds up one of my many neckties, pulling it taut in her fists and crumpling the forest green silk beyond repair.

"We skipped Day 12," she says.

Day 12 was *bondage*.

I groan and flop back onto the pillows. "How about we start with you?"

"Nope! *You* didn't participate in the blindfold prompt, so you're technically in breach. I suggest you mitigate damages."

"I love when you use legal jargon in bed." I reach for her but she rolls away.

"Don't distract me. I have big plans for you. Get up."

Valencia insists our plaid pajamas aren't the right attire, but I loaned my Rudolph harness to Rodrigo and I'm fresh out of additional BDSM gear. She finally concedes that black underwear will have to do. I slip into silk boxers, and she puts on her black bra and the satiny panties I'd unpacked into the dresser. She slicks her curly hair into a high ponytail and completes the ensemble with red lipstick and black ankle boots.

When I see her, I almost swallow my tongue.

"You were right," I choke out. "This is way better."

Since we skipped two holiday-related activities on our list, she demands that we incorporate Christmas somehow. She strolls through the living room like an off-duty dominatrix, then snaps her fingers.

"I've got it. Come over here."

She holds a long red ribbon—a leftover from Day 5—and I assume she's going to tie me to the bed, but she has something else in mind. In short order, I'm lying under the Christmas tree, my wrists secured to the trunk with my green silk tie and the red ribbon wrapped around my neck like a bow.

"I would like to once again express my reservations about this." If she tickles me, there's an extremely high chance I'm going to bring this nine-foot tree down on our heads.

"Don't be a wuss."

She disappears into the kitchen and I listen hard. Is that the freezer drawer? Sure enough, she returns with an ice cube in her hand.

I clench my fists on the tie. "Valencia—"

"Shh." She holds a finger to her lips and begins a slow, sultry strut toward me. Despite my misgivings, my cock starts to stir. By the time she reaches me, I'm hard as a fucking rock.

She kneels between my legs and puts her hand to her mouth in faux surprise.

"Santa left me a present under the tree." She adopts a breathy voice that's so ridiculous, I don't know whether to laugh or to beg. "I'd better unwrap it and see what it is."

Then she slips the ice cube into her mouth and reaches for the waistband of my boxers.

Beg. I'm definitely going to beg.

"Oh, fuck. Vixen, *please*—"

The sound of my apartment door opening is so unexpected, it takes me a moment to identify it.

"Wait," I hiss, trying to peer around Valencia. She notices my distress and climbs off me. A horrified squeak emerges from her throat, and I probably make a similar sound, because there, at the other end of the room, stands Andrea Noble.

My *mother*.

It's ten in the morning, but she's runway ready in a long white coat and black stilettos. I've always thought she looked like a taller Marion Cotillard with a short, wavy bob. Sharp green eyes, the same ones she passed down to me, sweep over us with an all-knowing gaze.

Me, tied to the fucking Christmas tree. And Valencia in her underwear and boots.

Mom sends us an arch look. "Is this why you couldn't come to Paris, Gideon? I didn't realize you were so . . . tied up."

Valencia opens her mouth and the ice cube falls out. It lands on my bare stomach, and I yelp at the sudden cold.

Someone else barges through the open door.

"Feliz Natal!" the stranger calls out, then he stops short, taking in the scene. His handsome—and oddly familiar—face breaks into a huge grin, and he turns to my mom. "You were right, minha vida. I think your son is *very* surprised."

Surprised doesn't even begin to cover it.

"Mom!" I shout, finally finding my voice. It cracks like I'm twelve years old. "What are you doing here?"

"Don't let me interrupt." She starts to stroll toward the kitchen, then stops and narrows her eyes.

Next to me, Valencia sucks in a breath. I know why—it looks like my mother is glaring at her, but really, the woman just hates wearing her glasses.

"Torres?" my mother asks, a note of disbelief in her tone. "Valencia Torres? Is that you?"

"Hi, Mrs. Noble," Valencia says weakly, waving a hand. "Um . . . Merry Christmas."

My mother's face breaks into a brilliant smile. "Please, my dear. Call me Andrea. Now, shall I let you two finish up?"

Valencia covers her face, and I yell, "You were supposed to be in Paris!"

Five minutes later, Valencia and I are wearing our matching pajamas and standing awkwardly in the kitchen with my mother and her guest.

Mom finally deigns to introduce him.

"This is Caio Pereira. We met during Paris Fashion Week. Caio's a model and photographer from Brazil."

That explains why he looks familiar. His tan face is striking, with narrow brown eyes, straight slashing brows, and high cheekbones. His loose brown curls are in desperate need of a cut.

He's also *much* younger than my mom. But it's been almost ten months since my father passed, and I can't imagine it was easy being Malcolm Noble's wife. She deserves to be happy.

However, she's also a wealthy widow, and I'll be looking this guy up the first chance I get.

Mom and Caio arrived with a ton of food, and she's busy selecting dishes from the cabinets. Caio makes espresso for all of us.

I'm rummaging in a drawer for tea, because Valencia prefers it, when I see my mother pull her aside. I strain my ears and watch out of the corner of my eye.

My mother takes Valencia's hand. "I heard about your parents, dear. I'm very sorry."

"Thank you. My condolences to you as well."

"Holidays are more difficult than other days, aren't they?" Mom says lightly. "It's more obvious that someone is missing."

My mother pats Valencia's shoulder, then carries a box of pastries to the dining table. Caio follows, balancing a tray of espresso cups.

The second they're gone, I stride over to Valencia. Her mouth is pink and swollen from scrubbing off the lipstick. I want to kiss her, but I'm worried about getting caught again.

"Are you all right?" I ask her.

She gives me a penetrating look. "Are *you*?"

"I guess." I glance over my shoulder at the doorway. "I just can't believe my mother is dating someone—"

"Younger?"

"Who doesn't brush his hair."

"Oh, stop."

"I'm serious. Why do you think I'm such a tyrant about mine?"

She grins and ruffles my hair, which I combed before she tied me to the tree. "Is that why you teased me for having messy hair when we were kids?"

I think about that for a moment. "I'll mention it to Ralph. It's possible I subconsciously equated wild hair with freedom, and secretly envied yours."

Her mouth twists wryly. "Mine is pretty wild."

"I like it. And I especially like it like this." I twine my fingers in her hair now. She's taken it down from the ponytail, and because she washed it last night, it's a long, alluring mass of dark curls instead of the straight, shiny curtain she prefers these days.

But even Valencia's hair can't distract me from the current situation, and I ask, "Do you think he's younger than we are?"

"I'm thirty-four."

I spin around, and Caio is standing right there, a wan smile on his face.

"I moisturize obsessively," he says. "And age is nothing but a number. Where do you want these?" He holds up a few gift bags and sends me a shit-eating grin. "Since it seems like the space under the tree is reserved for something else."

Valencia groans, but I can't help laughing. I like this guy.

We spend a surprisingly nice Christmas with my mother and Caio. Valencia calls her grandparents in Florida, and Rodrigo sends me an all-caps text, demanding updates. I forbid Valencia from telling him anything.

She raises her eyebrows. "Is your work husband the jealous type?"

"No, but I gave him shit when Bailey moved in after a week, and he'll never let me live this down."

She pats my chest. "We'll hold off on the press release."

After breakfast, I join Valencia for her volunteer shift at a food kitchen, then we swing by her apartment to pick up Archimedes. In a move that shocks everyone, my mother scoops Archie into her arms and smothers him with kisses. Even more shocking? Archie *allows* it.

By the time Mom and Caio leave, it's 10:00 p.m. and Valencia is yawning.

"One last thing," I tell her. "Then you can sleep."

"I'm fine." She immediately yawns again. "Okay, maybe I'm a little tired. What's the one last thing?"

Taking her hand, I draw her over to the mantel. On the day we decorated, Valencia hung two stockings there, as I did in her apartment. These are mint green satin with embroidered white snowflakes, and she said they reminded her of my eyes.

"This one is yours." I hand her the one on the left.

"And this one is yours." She gives me the second stocking.

I frown as I pull out a sealed red envelope. "When did you put this in here?"

"Monday." She smiles. "Open it."

"We'll open them together."

We sit on the sofa, and as he did that first night, Archimedes lumbers into the room and wedges himself between us. He immediately flexes his claws into the leather, and I sigh.

So it begins.

Valencia pulls out a small, square origami box.

"Did you make this?" When I nod, she gazes at it like it's something precious. "On the count of three? One, two . . ."

"Three." I slit open the envelope.

Inside, there's a card that reads, "All I want for Christmas is you . . . naked!" Smiling, I open it and find a sheet of paper ripped from a spiral notebook—the same one, I'm sure, that we wrote our list in. I unfold it and read Valencia's spiky script.

Dear Gideon,

I forgive you. But more importantly, please know that you're allowed to forgive yourself. You learned from your mistakes and you changed, which is more than most people ever do.

The truth is, you're a good man. (And extremely hot.) I wish we could've been friends in school, but I'm happy we found each other now.

Have a nice life. I hope I get to be part of it.

Love,

Valencia

P.S. Any interest in a Valentine's Day list?

The breath catches in my lungs. I read the letter three times before focusing on the first sentence.

I forgive you.

I'm not sure I realized how much I needed to hear this. From *her*.

Except . . . she's right. Her forgiveness doesn't relieve the weight of my past completely. All this time, I've been afraid of becoming like my father, but that very fear ensured that I wouldn't. So the burden I've carried about whether or not to forgive him . . .

Has actually been about forgiving *myself.*

The simplicity of that strikes me like a blow. What if I *am* allowed to forgive myself? What would the rest of my life look like if I did?

I lift my gaze to Valencia sitting beside me with a cranky cat tucked between us. This, right here, is what I could have.

If I just let the past go and spend the rest of my life being the person she sees in me.

She appears to be equally speechless, staring open-mouthed at the set of keys I've gifted her. She rubs her thumb over the cutesy acrylic key chain.

"Is this a Scottish fold cat?"

"That's what he is, right?" I scratch my fingers down Archie's back and direct my next words to him. "Would've been a lot easier if you were an orange tabby. I had to beg an Etsy seller in Iowa to express ship it."

Valencia puts down the keys and buries her face in her hands. I glance up in alarm.

"What's wrong?" After this roller coaster of a day, I can't decipher her reaction.

Her voice is muffled as she speaks into her palms. "Gideon, ever since my parents died, I've worried about being a burden to the people around me. This year, especially, I felt like I didn't belong anywhere. With anyone. *To* anyone." She raises her head, and even though her eyes are glassy with tears, she's smiling. The warmth of it lights up my soul. "But since the moment I saw you, I haven't felt alone."

"Because you *do* belong. Here, with me." I say it seriously so she knows I mean it. "Call it coincidence or Christmas magic, but when I saw you at that club, I knew we were being given a second chance. I'll never take that, or you, for granted. You're not a burden, Valencia Torres. You're a *gift*."

She lets out a choked sob and pulls me into a hug. The cat gives a loud, annoyed meow but doesn't move. We both laugh and settle for sharing a kiss over his head.

Easing back, I add, "That's a yes, by the way. To being part of my life, *and* to making a Valentine's Day list."

Her eyes hold a wicked gleam, and I can't wait for whatever genius ideas she has in store for us.

Valencia and Gideon's Naughty and Nice List might be over, but our life together is just beginning.

Author's Note

Thank you to Sarah E. Younger, Maria Gomez, and Lindsey Faber—an absolute dream team!

I originally wrote *The Holiday Hookup List* for a different project, and I'm thrilled that we were able to bring Valencia and Gideon's super-steamy love story to readers. This is my *sixth* short holiday romance, and honestly, I never get tired of writing these!

If you're looking for the others, *Only Santas in the Building* is available in KU and as part of the *Under the Mistletoe* collection. I also worked on two stories in *Amor Actually*, a holiday romance anthology featuring interconnected stories from seven Latina romance authors. *Solstice Miracle* is free for newsletter subscribers, and *Dance All Night* is a stand-alone holiday novella set in the world of *The Dance Off*.

Thank you so much for reading, and please consider leaving a review.

Newsletter

Subscribe to Alexis Daria's author newsletter to receive exclusive content, including a bonus epilogue for *The Holiday Hookup List*!
https://alexisdaria.com/newsletter/

About the Author

Alexis Daria is the award-winning and internationally bestselling author of *Along Came Amor*, *You Had Me at Hola*, *Take the Lead*, and more. Her books have been featured on several "best of" lists and have received starred reviews from multiple trade publications. A former visual artist, Alexis is a lifelong New Yorker who loves Broadway musicals and pizza. For more information, visit www.alexisdaria.com.